Resident Alien
And Other Stories

RESIDENT ALIEN AND OTHER STORIES

AN ANTHOLOGY OF IMMIGRANT VOICES FROM
AFRICA AND THE AFRICAN DIASPORA

Edited By

ADA UZOAMAKA AZODO
AND
AKACHI ADIMORA-EZEIGBO

GOLDLINE AND JACOBS PUBLISHING
GLASSBORO + NEW JERSEY

GOLDLINE AND JACOBS
PUBLISHING

Published in the United States
By Goldline and Jacobs Publishing
10 Franklin Road
P. O. Box 714, Glassboro,
New Jersey, 08028, USA

Resident Alien and Other Stories
Copyright Ada Uzoamaka Azodo & Akachi Adimora-Ezeigbo 2020
The moral rights of the editors/authors have been asserted
Database right Goldline and Jacobs Publishing (maker)

First Published 2020
All Rights Reserved
No part of this publication may be reproduced, stored in a retrieval system or transmitted in any form or by any means electronic, mechanical, photocopying, recording or otherwise without the permission of the publishers.

Cover Art: Antique Janus Face, an African Ceremonial Mask, Vintage African Art @elcidgallery

ISBN: 978-1-938598-41-8

Library of Congress Control Number: 2020934110

Printed in the United States of America

Alexa and the other guests, perhaps even Georgina,
All understood the fleeing from the war,
From the kind of poverty that crushed human souls,
But they would not understand the need to escape
From oppressive lethargy of choicelessness.
They would not understand why people like him
Who were raised well fed and watered but mired in dissatisfaction,
Conditioned from birth to look towards somewhere else,
Eternally convinced that real lives happened in that somewhere else,
Were now resolved to do dangerous things, illegal things,
So as to leave,
None of them starving, or raped, or from burned villages,
But merely hungry for choice and certainty.

---Chimamanda Ngozi Adichie, *Americanah*

CONTENTS

Introduction: A First Fruit of the Harvest Season	1
Tomi Adeaga	
One: Mirage	9
Two: The Expired Welcome	15
Akachi Adimora-Ezeigbo	
Three: Dilemma of a Senior Citizen	25
Four: Out of Sight	39
Omofolabo Ajayi-Soyinka	
Five: Resident Alien	51
Six: Peas A' Pod	59
Ada Uzoamaka Azodo	
Seven: Her Purple Huffy	83
Eight: A Wake in Chytown	93
Pede Hollist	
Nine: A Life of Solitude	107
Ten: The First-Place Poem Defense	115
Naana Banyiwa Horne	
Eleven: Miimi Is Being Bad Again	127
Twelve: Reconnected Redefined	141
H. Oby Okolocha	
Thirteen: The Londoner Goes Home	165
Fourteen: Travel Ban	169

Introduction: A First Fruit of the Harvest Season

Ada Uzoamaka Azodo &
Akachi Adimora-Ezeigbo

A FIRST FRUIT OF THE HARVEST SEASON! Hardly are those words out than they conjure up an image of women and men tilling the soil, hoeing, planting, and pruning in a farm, and afterwards reaping, garnering and gathering the yield into a barn. Indeed, by its very backward design this anthology breaks the state of inviolability of the field. It is an offering to the African gods of creativity, in this instance Ghanaian, Nigerian, and Sierra Leonean, with whom all things are possible. The writers of the short stories in this collection owe everything to them.

Some parts of this collection, like diverse produce at Harvest time, can be tart or succulent. Still, the Immigrant Short Stories Group of the African Literature Association of America, after over a decade of toil and moil, is glad to bring forth the first in a series of recorded experiences lived, observed, memorialized, or (re)imagined. For even as Zora Neale Hurston put it, "There is no agony like bearing an untold story inside you."

This assortment of stories can generate different emotions, too. As narratives they do provide insights into the human condition, especially when one is away from home yet does not quite feel at home in the new place of residence. They mirror how the environment impacts the individual at any stage of life and in diverse spaces. Owing to their complexity and depth, they might urge the reader to embrace a given writer and learn a thing or two about life. Indeed, these are fascinating and intriguing stories that portray shifting identity, personality, and inability to make sense of the reality lived or living at a particular point in time.

Some of the stories could inspire the reader and be the cause of her or his joy and laughter. Then again, other stories could challenge the reader and cause significant discomfort, despair, and fear of life. Nonetheless, the stories have allowed their writers the opportunity to gain distance and the necessary space for reflection, learning and teaching. Having gained the ability to consider human innermost impulses, thoughts, triumphs and failures, the writers have provided the reading public with a particular lens with which to peer through and examine human experiences.

At one end of the spectrum are stories on immigrant life and living in Europe. Tomi Adeaga's "Mirage" and "The Expired Welcome" portray life in the diaspora as a frequent disappointment and frustration, reminiscent of the ordeals of the mythical Tantalus and Sisyphus at the hands of the all-powerful gods sans merci. Akachi Adimora-Ezeigbo's "Dilemma of a Senior Citizen" and "Out of Sight" realistically mirror immigrant life in a quagmire and at critical moments when the immoral side of the psyche sends impulses to partake of the 'forbidden fruit' at the same time that the moral side urges decorum and flight away from the devil and all his sins. H. Oby Okolocha's "The Londoner Goes Home" is reflective of unfulfilled immigrant life in a labyrinth, where the neophyte's progress and spiritual march forward is persistently thwarted, abandoning him in an unending maze.

At the other end of the spectrum is a larger swath of stories with a focus on life and living in North America. "Resident Alien" by Omofolabo Ajayi-Soyinka announces the dread of the eternal immigrant, often misjudged as an out-of-space alien, a specter, a shade drifting around and so merits no respect or consideration for her or his personality and self-identity. Then, in "Peas A' Pod," a veritable syncopated piece of jazz, metaphorically speaking, Ajayi-Soyinka takes the reader through highs and lows, off, between and round discordant beats and rhythms that finally drop into a sacred dance bemoaning the ill-fortune of self-exile that does not spare its victim's integrity, self-dignity or self-identity. Two child-oriented stories palliate the reader, and compel her or him to see life with a child's eye; they reflect the perspective of children on existential cum philosophical topics of satiety and happiness. In "Her Purple Huffy," Ada Uzoamaka Azodo strategizes survival, even endurance, through the mere adoption of a child's unmitigated positive attitude to life. In "Miimi is Being Bad Again," Naana Banyiwa Horne fields a child protagonist still in a state of innocence, who questions quotidian observations in order to understand them, in contrast to adult despair, distress, fear, disappointment and desperation before the same experiences and problems. No longer are the youngsters' demands to be heard invisible, for children *do* have their own world of survival and endurance that is quite recommendable and distinct from that of adults. Nonetheless, Horne's "Reconnected Redefined" explores adult defiance of loss and trauma, through a focus on cultivating coping abilities, developing a new sense of community, and refusing to accept failure as an option. Then, Azodo's "A Wake in Chytown" recalls the folly of human behavior when funeral hoppers look out for their own personal pleasure and pecuniary satisfaction at the expense of the bereaved. In Pede Hollist's "A Life of Solitude," echoes of the aftermaths of the horrid Vietnam War reverberate; the isolation of the varied and hybrid offspring of that violent and traumatic experience, their poverty and mixed emotions, and their struggles for survival that sometimes lead them to crimes, criminals and criminality. Next, in "The First-Place Poem Defense" Hollist poetically and rhetorically juxtaposes life's struggles between conflicting and irreconcilable cultures of origin and the diaspora. Finally, Okolocha's "Travel Ban" explores interpersonal gender war several thousand feet up above in an airplane. It takes immigration check on the ground to recall the travelers to their shared destiny in the eventuality of a plane crash. Heretofore temporarily oblivious of their mortality, they then confront the tyranny of their common future as beleaguered immigrants in the hostland.

Suffice it to say that together the stories in *Resident Alien and Other Stories* constitute a coterie of illuminations and enlightenment on the human condition. In writing from the margin, the authors have designed an inventive strategy of three goals to dramatize certain aspects of human nature. The first goal is to contribute to the growing body of uncommon voices. The second goal is to illustrate how human actions betray human thoughts. The third goal is to mirror minority experiences of transnational border crossing discourses. Through the various additions to personal or (re)imagined authorial perspectives on creative literary representations, the anthology seeks to update already existing insights into the nature of lives in diverse places in the postcolonial cum postmodern times, while underpinning the challenges, trials and tribulations of traveling away from one's place of birth to the diaspora.

Each contributor has provided two primary sources that undergird knowledgeable and enlightened investigation into issues of identity, personality, and reconstruction in times of travel, immigration crises, exile, bigotry, institutionalized discriminations, misogyny, subjectivity and agency, and healing and coping. Among the relevant theories that could facilitate the reading and study of the stories is, first and foremost, the soundscape concept. With this approach to literary analysis, readers employ super-sensory reading of the environmental space. Among the subjects of analysis are audible and inaudible sounds; human voices and human silences; dreams, daydreams, soliloquies, and thoughts; (interior)monologues; listening and eavesdropping; laughter, crying, wailing, and screams; sighs and sobbing; music, dancing, singing, chanting, clapping, and computer renditions; television; airplanes taking off, flying and landing; ceiling fans blowing; trains running; electricity generators humming; gunshots; road traffic and car horns; pidgin and vernacular, all mirroring in special ways the complex, contradictory and complicated immigrant life and living in the diaspora. Such a sonic and oblique reading of the text could extend and deconstruct the didactic ending with a moral lesson often associated with the very nature and structure of the short story, revealing a more sophisticated textual interpretation and meaning. A gender approach could also serve the readers of these short stories. Through employing indigenous African feminist theories, such as Womanism, Woman palavering, Stiwanism, Nego-feminism, Motherism, Femalism, Snail-sense feminism, Di-feminism, Focu-feminism, and Satanism, readers could unearth new layers of meaning. Above all, together, the theories provide intersectional insights and views that make identity issues and the politics of difference and location subjects of feminist discourse, facilitating thereby psychoanalytic and traumatic approaches to the study of these postmodern and postcolonial literary texts.

The structure of this anthology is such that a critic could choose to work on the entire volume as a whole, yet be able to choose to study, analyze and interpret one given author only, or compare and contrast two, three or more authors and their stories.

What is more, while reading the stories, the reader has a chance to see if there is room to reconsider the world reality, admit mistakes that might have been made in the past, and even correct some of them. In other words, the stories urge the reader to do more than merely read, but also in studying them to judge less the people one comes across every day in her or his neighborhood. Indeed, they suggest the imperative of being flexible and adaptable, not rigid and fixed, according someone you meet some dignity, not just tolerating her or him, and respecting and valuing the person she or he is in a truthful and meaningful manner.

This anthology should be of interest to all educators as an addition to the curriculum in the Humanities colleges of their universities. It could provide useful and invaluable texts to guide the youth in lifelong learning, as well as direct their experiences as they search for higher order ways of thinking, behaving, and achieving a sense of order. Generally, it illuminates human behavior and enlightens the reading public about love, and such other less than perfect emotions as hatred, frailty, and desire, all of which emotions are opportunistic, conflicting, and complicated humanity attributes that come through in this story collection. According to Howard Zinn, peace activist, historian and author, on changing peoples' lives, "We don't have to engage in grand, heroic actions to participate in the process of change. Small acts, when multiplied by millions of people, can transform the world."

Tomi Adeaga

Tomi Adeaga Ph.D. teaches African literature in the Department of African Studies, Faculty of Philological and Cultural Studies, University of Vienna, Austria. Her areas of interest include African literature studies, translation studies, as well as Afro-European studies. Adeaga has published, with Sarah Udoh-Grossführtner, *Payback and Other Stories: An Anthology of African and African Diaspora Short Stories* (2018). Adeaga is also the author of *Translating and Publishing African Language(s) and Literature(s): Examples from Nigeria, Ghana and Germany* (2006), and a short story titled "Marriage and Other Impediments" in *African Love Stories: An Anthology*, edited by Ama Ata Aidoo (2006). Adeaga translated Olympe Bhêly-Quénum's *C'était à Tigony* into English as *As She Was Discovering Tigony* (2017). Adeaga has also published book chapters and literary articles in academic journals. Adeaga serves on several editorial boards of academic journals, including the *Journal of African Gender Studies (JAGS)*, and *Stichproben: Vienna Journal of African Studies*.

One

Mirage

MY WOES BEGAN THE DAY I WAS born. My first sound was a cry of despair. It was as if my tiny self, I, Tinuola (Tinu) Thomas, the only child of Bamidele and Banke Thomas, could see into the future and I did not want to come out of my mother's womb. My parents occupied prominent positions as philanthropists in the Nigerian community in particular and the black community in general in Germany. My dad made his money from the numerous projects that he accomplished for oil industries across the world, such as Shell, Elf, and Mobil, to name only a few. We were often cited as the perfect family by members of the black community. But it was all a mirage!

As an only child, I spent most of my childhood jostled between my grandparents in Lagos, Nigeria, and my parents' housemaids in Berlin. My grandparents spoiled me and made up for the love that I never received at home. They were both parents and grandparents to me. Our housemaids in Berlin were the only ones who talked to me when I was at home. My dad was always away on one business or another; Tokyo today, and South Africa tomorrow…. It was quite difficult to keep up with his movements. He loved being everywhere else but at home.

Mom was a country club mom, so to say; she had her own group of friends with whom she spent more time socializing than caring for me. They either talked about the *Owambe* Nigerian party that they were going to organize for some visiting dignitary from Nigeria or about how they were going to dress up for the occasion. At other times, they would discuss which holiday location to choose for their next vacation, the more expensive the better. After all, their husbands and boyfriends were going to pay for them. When my mother was not socializing, she was quarreling with my dad. They fought constantly, and this over everything.

Dad would scream at her when she came in through the door, "Why are you coming home at this time of the day? Who is that man who dropped you off just now?"

Mom would retort, "What? Do I have to take permission from you before I go out? Why do you want to know who dropped me off? Do I ask you about what you do with your life?"

"What nonsense? You are my wife, and I have every right to know who dropped you off," Dad would insist.

Many times he would follow up with slapping my mom. She would threaten to call the police, if he did not leave her alone. She would brandish her cellphone, and the ploy always worked, because he would storm out of the house, jump into his car and drive away. I never knew when he came back late in the night. It was such that whenever he treated her badly and beat her up, she took it out on me by beating me, ignoring me and pretending that I was not even there. It took me a long time to realize that the reason Mom treated me this way was because I was a carbon copy of my dad. I grew up thinking that everything that went wrong in our family was my fault. So, on the outside, she always behaved as if everything was alright. But, owing to her position of importance in the Nigerian community, she did not want to become an object of ridicule. You see, our people can be very nasty when it comes to destroying one's reputation.

Ours was indeed a dysfunctional family, a mirage. One day, at about 8 years of age, I was supposed to spend the afternoon with my best friend, Annika, but I came straight back home from school, because she took ill that morning and did not even come to school. After having had lunch and done my homework, I was hearing some low voices downstairs. I crept to the top of the railings and from there I saw my dad talking with someone who could not have been much older than me, a child between 12 and 13 years old. I was going to go back to my room, when I saw them go into my parents' bedroom. I was curious, so I peeped through the keyhole. Lo and behold, I saw my dad and the boy having sex. Out of fear of my dad, who might think that I was spying on him, I had to cover my mouth so as not to scream. I curled up in my bed and went into a state of shock. I wetted my bed and stayed like that until the next day. When I did not come out of my room the next morning, my mom came to drag me out of my bed. She screamed at me for having wetted my bed and for not getting ready for school. But, seeing that I was unresponsive, she took me to the hospital. At the hospital, they found nothing wrong with me.

Mom scolded me, again, when we got home, thinking that I was trying to play truancy. "Go to your room," she screamed at me. "And know that you are going to school tomorrow."

For the next 5 years, Dad found creative ways to bring his boys home when Mom was out. He never realized that I knew his dirty secret, which dirty secret even at 13 years of age was still a huge weight to carry around on my shoulders. I was not bold enough to share this secret with anybody, because no one would have believed me. On the other hand, I started resenting my Dad's touch. He thought that I was just being difficult, stubborn and ill-mannered. I threw a lot of tantrums at home, fought with my classmates in school, and skipped classes. My teachers would call my dad to report my behavior to him, warning that I would be sent out of school, if nothing was done about my bad behavior. Of course, on such occasions, Dad vented his anger on my mom, screaming at her.

"Banke, come and see how your daughter is misbehaving. Instead of staying home to raise her up to be a well-behaved and respectful daughter, you spend time shopping with your useless friends."

"And you *nko*? Why can't you spend some time with her? When did you last do something with her? Have you ever taken her to the park? Do you even know her friends? No, you don't. Dele, we are not in Nigeria where you can hide behind your servants and relatives. Here, in this country, we are equal partners. I will do what I want."

This back and forth would go on and on for some time. Afterwards, they would simply walk out of the house and drive away in different directions, claiming that they had appointments to keep. When we went out to church on Sundays, we were like one happy family. But, as soon as the doors of the church shut behind us, we were like strangers to one another. So, I ended up finding relief in my own imaginary world where there was no pain. I would stay in my room and read my books all day. I only came out to the kitchen to eat and talk to the housemaid.

The most interesting part of it all, which was difficult for me to swallow, was our annual Christmas parties in which Dad displayed his wealth to the rest of the African community. He always made sure that he invited ambassadors, visiting ministers, and prominent black entrepreneurs in Germany. After the obligatory meet-and-greet, women wished their own husbands could be as caring as my dad and that their own children were as obedient and intelligent as I. I would run to my room and would not come out until the following day.

That was the hell in which I grew up; a make-believe family, a mirage. I grew quite lean and often walked around with my head in the clouds. One day, I collapsed in my American literature class and was rushed to the hospital. There, the attending doctor referred me to a psychologist for evaluation. The psychologist told me that I was in a state of depression, adding that I had to snap out of it or face schizophrenia, the next and worse stage of depression, which was going to be extremely difficult to cure.

"Tell me about yourself," the psychologist urged me, gently.

That was how I came to relate my story to the psychologist after the third meeting. She wanted to see my parents and, having obtained my permission, invited them to accompany me to the next meeting with her.

After we were all seated, the psychologist asked them to listen to my story. I took a deep breath and unburdened myself of my story. Mom let out a heart-rending scream and broke down crying. She was confronted with a part of her husband's life that she had suspected, but refused to believe was true. Dad buried his head in his hand and could not look at me in the face. He stayed that way until the psychologist came to tap his hand, telling him to sit up. He did so, brushing the tears away from his eyes with the back of his hand. Mom sat up straight, like a statue, as if she was in a state of shock.

"Now that you have both listened to her for the first time in her life, you must all heal together as a family. This is the only opportunity for you to do so, otherwise, you will lose her," said the psychologist, going back to her seat.

"Yes, but before we go on, I am terribly sorry for hurting you, my child. I never knew that I was the source of your problems. Forgive me, Tinuola, forgive me," begged my dad. Then, turning to my mom, he stretched out his hand and clasped hers and looking into her eyes asked her for forgiveness as well.

"Forgive me, Banke. I have been the worst husband and father. I have brought so much havoc into your life and forgot the vows we made to each other when we got married. Let us work together to heal as a family."

For the first time in my life, we hugged one another and wept together as a family.

Two

The Expired Welcome

WHEN I WAS A CHILD, I WATCHED repeatedly *Sound of Music* (1965), a Nazi-era musical drama film about an Austrian family, the von Trapps. I learnt all the words of the songs by heart. I felt I was in love with the German language and culture. I always wanted to learn to speak German, so I spent a lot of time at the Goethe Institute library in Lagos, Nigeria. I applied to Universities in Germany and Austria and was admitted to the Johann Wolfgang Goethe University, Frankfurt am Main, Germany, to study International Relations. For me, Teniola Oyenuga, studying in Germany was the fulfillment of a dream come true. But, at no time in my dream did I think of going to study or live in Canada! But, here I am *en route* to Ottawa, Canada, to start a new job! How did that happen?

It's been seven years since I came to study in Germany. Honestly speaking, I can't believe that I have finally completed the studies for both my Bachelor of Arts and Master of Arts degrees in International Relations at the university. Looking back now, I remember how difficult it was for me to learn the German language. We were a group of foreigners that first of all had to go through the language school. That was the most interesting part of my studies at the university, because it was like a scene out of the old British comedy, *Mind Your Language*.

"Herr Chan! Ich spreche kein Chinesisch!" (Mr. Chan! I do not speak the Chinese language!)

The teacher always targeted the Chinese guy, who was unable to pronounce German words correctly. Whenever the poor guy started reading a text, the teacher would interrupt him, screaming that she did not speak Chinese. There was so much laughter in that class! I spent most of my free time sitting in front of the television in my hostel to learn German, which I then practiced on my German boyfriend, Fabian Himmelreich. In a minute, I will tell you more about Fabian.

***

Well, since I was not on scholarship, I had to work hard to pay my school fees and rent. I was, therefore, happy to have completed my studies within seven years. What I did not know was that my problems were just starting, for trying to get a job within the one year period of grace that I was given by the foreign office officials after my studies, as stated in the law, proved to be a great challenge. I sent quite a large number of applications to international organizations across the country and even to England, the U.S.A., Canada, and other countries. But, nobody in Germany wanted to employ a noncitizen. I got in touch with some headhunters in Britain and the response I received was the same, nothing, nothing, nothing.

The laws in the U.S.A. had changed considerably since the 9/11 bombing. I applied for a highly professional program, but my application had not yet been processed, due to the high number of applications they had to plough through. And, I feared that by the time they were finally ready, I would have been kicked out of Germany! I would have been constrained to go back home, where I knew my future was also uncertain. But, as the Germans would say, *"wer nicht wagt, der gewinnt nicht,"* meaning, if you don't try, you never know whether you will succeed. No pain, no gain!

When I later moved into a tiny apartment in another part of the city, I was the only black person in my neighborhood and it meant that everyone knew me. I also attracted a lot of scrutiny, for I kept being asked the same questions that every foreign, read black, student was likely to be asked.

Woher kommst du? Also, aus Nigeria? Wo genau liegt das? Ist es in der Nähe von Südafrika? Wann geht's du wieder nach Hause?

(Where are you from? Okay, from Nigeria? Is it near South Africa? When are you going back home?)

So, being 'exotic' meant that you had to endure such questions and either responded to them or walked away. I simply always walked away....

Now back to the episode of Fabian Himmelreich. And add to the problems of work and housing the issue that Fabian's family never took to me. Fabian's father was a rich industrialist that wielded a lot of influence in the region's government. He and Fabian's mother did not want their only child going out with a black girl. They had other plans for him; to marry a nice girl from a nice German home. At the disastrous first meeting, Fabian's dad's disdain for me and everything black was evident and literally palpable.

"Why are you going out with our son?" he asked me point blank.

"Because I love him," I replied.

"Blacks are not capable of loving anyone, they don't have emotions," he retorted.

"Yes, you're right," I responded, sarcastically, of course. "Black people are extraterrestrial beings from another planet." Then I walked away and went to sit in the car. We left shortly afterwards, Fabian and I, and I never went back there.

I kept writing applications for work, but all of them came back without any positive response. As the end of the one year of grace kept drawing nearer and nearer, I started entertaining the thought of going back home to Nigeria, again. But, there was a problem there, too. Having started a new life in Germany, I did not know what I would do there. Still, if I did nothing, I would surely be deported, sent back to Nigeria. What was I supposed to do? As if privy to my pseudo soliloquy Bridgette, my Cameroonian best friend, asked poignantly, "But, why not get married to Fabian and get an easy permanent residency?"

"No! That is the last thing I would ever want to do. I would rather relocate to another country. Then, if I still want to marry him I will do so on my terms," I responded.

"What if they deport you before then?" Bridgette asked me again.

"Well, that is the chance that I have to take," I again responded.

***

One day, I received a call for an interview with HOPE, an international organization in Frankfurt. I was overjoyed and could not sleep the night before the interview, although I fully prepared for it. Upon getting to their office on the day of the interview, I was ushered into a room. I did an excellent job answering appropriately all the questions that I was asked, I believed. But, a few days later, to my disappointment, I received a call that was later followed by a letter, saying that I did not make it because I was not the type of candidate they were looking for. To think that someone there actually called me and told me that I was the best candidate, but the interviewer wanted a white person! That was the pattern that most of the other applications also followed. It was such a devastating experience for me. What was I going to do next?

A few months later, Fabian asked me to marry him. He told me he loved me and could not live without me. I also told him that I loved him, but added that I was not yet ready to get married to him. The reason why I was reluctant to get married to Fabian under those circumstances was that getting married to a foreigner always raised a lot of suspicions in the community center; the officials there often did not believe that such marriages were based on love. They made that obvious by separately interviewing mixed couples and even trying to convince the German fiancé or fiancée not to marry a foreigner. All these demeaning practices were enough to put me off from marrying Fabian immediately. But, Fabian would not give up. He kept asking me to marry him and I kept holding him off. In fact, we almost broke up during the whole sordid situation.

But Fabian pressed on. He wore me down until I finally succumbed. When we went to the community center to apply for a marriage license, the official there thought it was an arranged marriage and told us so, adding that we were not going to be given a marriage license. We were told to prove that we were really in love. The proofs that they demanded were so many that the application dragged on for months. That was when I again started thinking of going back to Nigeria. But, this time, there was a new problem; I could not afford to leave Fabian behind. He was also strongly against my going back to Nigeria. Then, he went back to the community center to see the official that we had met when we applied for a marriage license. He was not there. Instead, there was a new face, a woman, who asked him if he had done something bad to someone higher up.

"It seems that someone has a problem with you getting married," she told Fabian.

"Why would anyone have a problem with me getting married? Whose business is it, anyway?"

"Well, I can see here that a Herr Himmelreich says that it is an arranged marriage, because the girl to whom you want to get married does not have a German nationality. Are you related to Herr Himmelreich?"

"Is the person's first name Harald?" Fabian asked.

"Yes, Harald, it is Harald. Why?"

"It must be my dad," Fabian told the woman. "Who else would be against my marriage?" Fuming, boiling over with anger, Fabian did not go back to his own home. Instead, he drove straight to his family home and confronted his parents with the information that he had just received. He threatened to walk out of their lives and never go back, if his dad did not release his stranglehold on the marriage license. Nothing happened, however. His dad did not change his mind.

***

Meanwhile, the time for me to leave Germany, if I did not get an employment, was drawing nearer. Both Fabian and I were getting jittery, but did not know what else to do. There were no responses from the international organizations that I had applied to in Canada. I was called for a few interviews for jobs for English speakers in companies based in cities across Germany, companies to which I had applied for work out of desperation. Each time I got there for an interview, I was either told that I was not the right candidate or that they needed a German national. This back and forth was weighing me down. With just three months left of my visa, the prospects of getting a marriage license was dimming. Since Fabian's dad did not back down from his stance, Fabian stopped taking his calls and refused to have anything to do with him. I was in a terrible emotional state. I dreaded the possibility of opening the door and finding the police in front of my house waiting for me with handcuffs!

One morning, as I was looking gloomily out of the window of my tiny apartment, the doorbell rang. Fabian's best friend, Kristof, stood there. He told me to come with him to the hospital, because Fabian had been involved in a serious car accident. I was going to run out in my pajamas, but he made me go back and change. I grabbed whatever I could for clothing and I ran out of my apartment with him. At the hospital, Fabian was in the intensive care unit and the following twenty-four hours were critical.

Fabian did not make it out alive from the intensive care. I broke down and wept bitterly. In my blurred vision, I saw his parents coming towards me. His mother was screaming wildly, saying that the *negerin* had killed her son. The nurses dragged her away, before she could get at me. Then, Kristof took me back home. He called Bridgette to come and stay with me before he returned to work.

The days that followed were like a nightmare. I was on the verge of committing suicide. I had nothing to live for again. So, I did not see the letter inviting me for an interview with the International Organization for Migration (IOM) in Berlin. I saw it only two days later and Bridgette encouraged me to go for it. She insisted on going with me to the interview. I honestly did not know what I said during that interview. Shortly after that, I also had a skype interview with another international organization in Ontario, Canada.

***

By now, I only had a month left to go back home. Fabian had been buried and his parents refused to let me attend his funeral and burial. I later went to his graveside and wept my heart out. I did not feel like going on. When my father suggested that I come back home after my visa expired, I did not argue.

Two days before my visa expired, I received a letter of a job offer with the IOM in Berlin. Under normal circumstances, I would have jumped up with joy, because it was what I had wanted, but I was numb, totally indifferent. I went on with my plans to leave Germany. And, just as Bridgette, who had been staying with me since Fabian's death, was packing my bags the day before I was to leave, I received another acceptance letter. This time, it was an offer to work with the IOM in Ottawa, Canada ....

Akachi Adimora-Ezeigbo

Akachi Adimora-Ezeigbo, Ph.D. poet, novelist, playwright, short story writer and children's literature author, feminist theorist of "Snail-Sense Feminism (2003)," a Fellow of Nigerian Academy of Letters (FNAL), Literary Society of Nigeria (FLSN), English Scholars Association of Nigeria (FESAN) and Association of Nigerian Authors (FANA), multiple award-winning writer and international scholar, was a Professor of English for thirty-five years at the University of Lagos. She has taught internationally at universities in South Africa and the United Kingdom and has delivered lectures in the United States, including Visiting Fellowships in the United Kingdom at School of Oriental and at African Studies (SOAS), University of London, in 1998/90, in South Africa at the University of Natal (now University of KwaZulu Natal) in Pietermaritzburg campus (1999/2000), in Germany at the Centre of African Studies, University of Bayreuth (2005), and at the Department of English, Royal Holloway University of London (2006/2007). Currently Ezeigbo teaches as a contract Professor at Alex Ekwueme Federal University Ndufu-Alike, Ikwo in South East Nigeria, while continuing her prodigious creative writing and activism in literary circles. Ezeigbo's literary awards include WORDOC Short Story Prize (1994), ANA/Spectrum Prize (2001), Zulu Sofola Prize (2002), Flora Nwapa Prize for Women's Writing (2003), ANA/Atiku Abubakar Children Literature Prize (2007), The Nigeria Prize for Literature (2007), ANA/Cadbury Prize for Poetry (2009); the Winner (First Prize) of the Creative Writing Prize for Short Story (Staff Category, 2019) and Winner (Second Prize) for Poetry (Staff Category, 2019, of Alex Ekwueme Federal University Ndufu-Alike(AE-FUNAI), Ikwo, and shortlisted for the Wole Soyinka Prize for African Writing (2012). Her other awards include Best Researcher Award in the Humanities at the University of Lagos (2005), a chieftaincy title –"Ugo Nwanyi Edemede Ndi-Igbo"–given by her people. Ezeigbo's over fifty books include *Fact and Fiction in the Literature of the Nigerian Civil War* (1991 & 2019) and *Gender Issues in Nigeria*.

THREE

DILEMMA OF A SENIOR CITIZEN

MARK HEAVED A SIGH OF RELIEF WHEN someone came for him at last. The cabin was almost empty as most of the passengers had left the aircraft except two elderly women and himself. He had sat quietly like an anthill, watching the disembarking men and women. Most of them were barely forty years old. After the plane came to a stop, they had risen, grabbed their pieces of luggage from the overhead lockers, ready to exit. Their energy almost frightened Mark. Most travelers in this part of the world were young people, he thought. It seemed elderly people stayed mostly at home. This was very much unlike the country from where he came. There, many of the passengers in most aircrafts were elderly people – men and women over sixty years old. People lived longer and had access to better health services, he supposed.

"Sir, I'm here to assist you to disembark," the airline staff said gently and waited patiently for Mark to make the first move.

"Thank you." Mark struggled to get up. His knees hurt and his lower back felt sore. He knew he should have got up more and walked around as his doctor advised, but it was not easy taking the walk along the passage with the crew and some passengers moving constantly. And it was worse when there was the mildest turbulence; then the plane became unstable. "I'm ready," he said, smiling at the young man.

Mark allowed the man to shepherd him out of the cabin. He observed two other people helping the two elderly women. Age is hard on the elderly, he thought sadly. Everything had become a struggle and he wondered how it would be when he got older. He was eighty at the moment. He leaned on the young man. "What's your name?" he asked.

"Stephen, sir."

"Thank you for this service, Stephen," he said.

"You're welcome, sir."

When they stepped out of the cabin, he saw three wheelchairs positioned by the side of the long passage that led to the building where immigration and customs officers were checking the passengers' international passports and luggage. It was a big plane and there were many passengers. Stephen assisted him to sit in one of the wheelchairs and began to push the chair carefully, following the exit sign. Mark knew he was not as feeble as he appeared at the moment. He was capable of getting around in Edinburgh, provided he took things easy and moved slowly. But the long flight and the long stretches of immobility stiffened his legs and strained his back. He told himself that he would feel much better once he had some rest. Onumba, his elder brother, had reassured him on the telephone and confirmed that good arrangement had been made to receive him. He had a choice to stay in Lagos or in Umuokpa, their village in the southeast of the country.

A fat woman, carrying a small hand luggage and a large jacket, waddled in front. Her long dress was too small for her size and there were bulges around her waist and buttocks. Mark stole a glance at her face as Stephen wheeled him past the struggling woman. He saw that she was young and wondered how she allowed herself to get to this size. Was it food? Wrong beverages? Lack of exercise? Mark wondered which was responsible. He brought his thoughts back to his homecoming, a decision he thought over carefully before taking it.

This was his second visit home since he left at the end of the Biafran War, over forty years ago. Mark couldn't explain to himself why he had not visited often or at least once in a while. He did not even come home when his father died, though he had managed to return briefly when his mother died some fifteen years ago. She followed her husband barely five years after he departed suddenly. Mark was told it was a heart attack that killed the old man. His mother died of breast cancer. Worse still, he never brought his two children home to see his people. His mother longed to meet her grandchildren, but Mark denied her the opportunity. Each time he thought about it now, he felt bad. He wept secretly. No one knew he did this; he wept only in the middle of the night when he was all alone. His weeping got worse after his retirement and as he grew weaker year by year.

At the immigration section, Mark got up from the wheelchair and took a step forward. He felt much better and thanked Stephen again as he wheeled the chair away. He was sure he could manage from this point. He had asked for the wheelchair to reduce the distance he would have to walk before collecting his luggage. "I am not crippled yet," he told himself with a smile. The queue for people with foreign passports was short and before long he was through with immigration checks. Collecting his one piece of luggage was easy, for there were people willing to help if paid a small fee. He engaged a young man with a funny haircut and bushy eyebrows, and he helped him to put his luggage in a trolley. The custom officers looked at him briefly and waved him on. The young man walked beside him, pushing the trolley as they headed for the exit.

Suddenly, Mark felt elated at the prospect of returning to his original home. In spite of everything, he was home and he hoped it was for a long time. Yes, he was finally home. No going back to the United Kingdom. No going back to Edinburgh. He was going to reunite with his two brothers, only sister, cousins, nieces and nephews and their families. So many new faces to see. All those born since he left. Some he met during his last visit, but he was almost sure he would not recognize many of them. He had to learn their names all over again. He hoped his memory would not fail him. He was aware that he was beginning to forget things. Yes, sometimes he forgot things, especially names. But he would be able to cope, he assured himself. Time was all he needed.

Outside the airport building, Mark saw so many people who came to meet their relations or friends or bosses. There were also people who asked if anyone needed a taxi or wanted to exchange currencies or buy recharge cards for their phones. He allowed his eyes to look around; Onumba had told him that one of his sons and his driver would meet him at the airport. So he looked around carefully to see if they had come for him. Not that he would know them, for he had not met either of them before. Then he saw a young man carrying a small cardboard on which his name was written. He smiled broadly and beckoned to the young man.

"I'm Mark Ude," he introduced himself. He removed his cap, revealing a head that was bald.

"Good evening, sir," the young man greeted him, bringing down his right hand that held the cardboard. "I'm Chidozie. My father asked me to fetch you. He said you knew I would be the one to pick you up from the airport." He was tall, dark-skinned and good-looking. He wore a short-sleeved shirt and blue jeans. A silver chain dangled from his neck and disappeared under his shirt.

Transferring his cap to his left hand, Mark stretched his hand and shook Chidozie's firmly. "I'm delighted to meet you, Chidozie."

"Is this your luggage?" Chidozie asked, turning to the man holding the trolley. When Mark nodded, Chidozie took over the trolley and began to push it forward, towards the car park.

"This way, Uncle," he said turning to Mark.

Mark thanked the man who had helped him and gave him some money. He put his wallet back in his pocket. Taking the money, the man smiled and closed his palm over it. "Thank you, sir." He walked back into the arrival hall. Mark followed his nephew to the car park, pleased that the first stage of his relocation to his original home was successful.

***

One week after he arrived in Lagos, Mark knew he could not live in the town everyone described as Nigeria's megacity. He was told that the population of Lagos was over thirty million. That was bigger than many countries in the world, he thought. He had arrived on a Friday and it took over three hours to get to Onumba's home in Lekki from the airport. A journey that ordinarily should take thirty minutes or less. The traffic was a mightmare. Chidozie kept apologizing and saying, "Sorry, Uncle, please try and get a nap if you feel like it. This is Lagos. Friday traffic is usually heavy." He had asked Chidozie not to worry about him, but before they got to Omoye Crescent in Lekki Phase One, Mark was drained of energy, distressed even. He had slept fitfully that night, because of the noise from the power generating sets in the neighboring houses.

"I hope you'll be able to sleep. There is power outage and everyone's generator is roaring away," Onumba had said, laughing. He had walked across to the Guest Chalet allocated to Mark to see how he was settling down. "Mind you, mine is one of them," Onumba had said, bursting into another bout of laughter. Though older than Mark by two years, Onumba looked younger than his brother.

"Don't worry, I'm so tired I'll drop off as soon as my head touches the pillow," Mark had replied, smiling. He saw that Onumba's sense of humor, which had marked him out in their youthful days, had remained intact in spite of his age and the vicissitudes of life in turbulent Nigeria.

"Well, good night then, my brother," Onumba said, getting up. "Welcome home, and feel comfortable in my home." He walked out of the room and shut the door gently. Seconds later, he was back and poked his head around the door. "Don't forget to lock the door."

Mark had stood up and locked the door. He sat down again and looked around. The Guest Chalet was beautiful and tastefully furnished. He got up and went to the window. The compound was large; the main house in which Onumba and his family lived was a four-bedroom terrace duplex with a massive standby power generating set. There were other facilities, including an elegant swimming pool. There were also boys' quarters and a security post. Mark shook his head, thinking aloud: "Onumba has really done well for himself. He is megarich."

It was a struggle to sleep that night, but at last he fell asleep and dreamt of his two grown children – his son in Glasgow and his daughter in Bristol.

Mma, Onumba's wife, tried to make Mark feel at home in Lagos, but it did not work out that way. She saw to it that everything was made available to help him settle down smoothly. She supervised the cook, who prepared good and appropriate meals suitable for his health condition. Mark was diabetic. Onumba employed a new driver and made a car available to Mark. Despite everything, the returnee found Lagos overwhelming and troubling.

Onumba took him out on Sunday for sightseeing. Mark sat beside Chidozie who was driving while Onumba and Mma sat at the back.

"Dozie will drive us today," Onumba said. "My driver has travelled to see his sick mother."

"That's okay," Mark said. "Chidozie is a good driver. I noticed that when he drove me to your house from the airport. And anyone who can drive in Lagos can drive easily in any part of the world."

Onumba threw his head back and laughed, his protruding belly shaking. Mma who was adjusting her headtie burst into laughter too. Mark found himself laughing with them. Chidozie merely smiled as he drove out of the open gate. The security man waited for the car to drive out and then locked the gate.

"That's what visitors always say after they've observed the traffic situation in Lagos," Onumba agreed. "There is some kind of crazy driving going on in Lagos all the time. Most drivers don't obey traffic regulations."

Mark had spent a week in Lagos now and was quite sure he did not wish to live there. He would die of stress and anxiety and pollution from the unhealthy fumes spreading carbon monoxide everywhere from power generating sets in people's houses and from cars trapped in unending traffic jams. He dreaded taking even the briefest of walks on the roads, because of the level of pollution and the way people drove carelessly. He had reached a decision to have a talk with Onumba to tell him about his predicament.

Onumba came over to the Guest Chalet after dinner. He wore a shirt and trousers made from adire material. "How are you my brother?" he asked, after settling his bulky frame in a chair opposite Mark.

"I'm good," Mark replied, nodding his head several times. "You and Mma have been spoiling me with comfort since I arrived. Good food, excellent accommodation – everything in this house exudes comfort."

"We can do no less, my brother. You have been away for so long and it is really great to have you back. As I told you, you can live with us permanently here in Lekki or you can move into one of our three-bedroom terrace houses with one bedroom boy's quarters located in a mini estate at Isheri. We can arrange for a nurse to care for you. Your family can visit you any time they wish..."

"Onumba, you're a wonderful brother and I am very grateful for all you have done to make me comfortable. And you have really done well in life. I congratulate you, my brother." Mark sat up and, folding the ample wrapper he tied around his waist, he pushed them gently between his slender thighs. "But there is a problem," he continued, hesitant, looking at Onumba sadly.

"A problem? What is the problem?" Onumba returned his gaze.

"I must tell you the truth. I cannot live in Lagos. I find the city overwhelming and disorienting. Life here is too fast for me. Too intense. The thought that I might live the rest of my life here frightens me. Perhaps I should go home and live in the village as you and Obioha suggested before I arrived in the country and when I mentioned that I would prefer a quiet life."

Onumba lifted his head and laughed. "Mark, is this what you call a problem? It's no problem, my brother. Yes, I remember well that our senior brother, Obioha, and I talked at length about your return home and agreed that you could stay near me in Lagos or move to the village where Obioha lives on our family land. As the first son of our late father, he chose to settle in the village in Umuokpa to warm and watch over our ancestral home."

"To preside at family meetings in the Obi," Mark said, smiling. He was delighted that Onumba did not object to his decision to leave Lagos and move to Umuokpa. "Let me say that my son and daughter would not like to visit Nigeria. They have no feeling for the country; perhaps it is my fault. I should have brought them for visits when they were younger. Both of them are married and have no desire to visit Nigeria or leave the United Kingdom. As you know, my British wife, Laura, and I are divorced. So I hardly have any strong family ties at the moment. My children are independent and when I became incapacitated, they suggested I move into a nursing home since I could not do most things for myself anymore. I told you all this; that was why I considered returning home. I disliked the idea of living in a nursing home, under care, losing my home and my independence."

"I don't blame you, my brother. The idea of living in such a place, in the midst of strangers and dependent on total strangers, is frightening for people like us who live in this country," Onumba said sympathetically.

Mark shook his head. His mind turned to his life in the United Kingdom where he spent the greater part of his life, toiling and raising his two children. They grew up, fell in love, got married and moved on with their lives. And Laura, the vivacious and beautiful woman he fell in love with in his student days and later married, chose to abandon him after twenty five years of marriage. What was her reason? She fell in love with a man she met in the local library in Addlestone. After their divorce, he could not bear to live in the small town anymore and relocated to Edinburgh. It all seemed a long time ago. And here he was, back to his original country.

"Remember I told you that Obioha and I had arranged things in such a way that if you chose to live in Umuokpa, that would not be a problem. A house is waiting for you there. Relations are hoping you would come. The service of a nurse was initially sought and then suspended until further notice. All we need to do now is to contact the nurse and renew our negotiation. So you have no problem, my brother," Onumba concluded with a grin.

"I don't know what to say." Mark raised both hands in amazement. "All I can say is that I do not deserve all this."

"We are a family. That is what matters." Onumba stood up. "Let me leave you, so you can get some sleep. Ka chi fo, good night."

Mark watched him leave the room and told himself that he did not deserve the kindness his brother was showing him, having ignored him and other relations for so many years.

***

There was a celebration the day Mark arrived in Umuokpa, accompanied by Onumba and Mma. They had flown to Enugu and chartered a vehicle to take them to Umuokpa. Obioha and his wife and a host of other relations were on hand to receive them in the Obi where Obioha received visitors and family meetings were held. It was a spacious room with low walls decorated with uri and other natural pigments women used to adorn homes in Umuokpa. There were chairs for almost everyone, but those who could not be accommodated in the Obi sat on chairs arranged outside, in front of the building.

Mark was touched by the warm reception. The main building stood a little distance from the Obi – a two-story modern house where Obioha and his family lived. There was a bungalow adjacent to it, which Mark was told was his new home.

After the breaking and eating of kolanut, Obioha addressed the gathering. "My people, we are happy to welcome our brother home. He has returned to his fatherland and we wish to welcome him. Our people say that the traveler must return home; Mark has returned home. Today is a memorable day; our ancestors are watching and I am sure they approve."

There was a loud ovation. While food and drinks were being served, Mark who wore a hat, a red and black isi-agu jumper and black trousers got up to address his relations – men and women. "My brothers and sisters and our wives, I thank you all. I appreciate this warm reception. It tells me that I am accepted by all of you, in spite of my years of absence from Umuokpa. I am happy to be home. I will participate in your meetings and join you in developing our community. Some of you I know and some I do not know, but it does not matter. We are one and, as our people say, when we urinate together, our urine will foam. I greet you all."

Some of the people wanted him to talk about his family, especially his children. They whispered among themselves. But Mark did not mention his family. After the feasting, people began to withdraw and return home. Only the two brothers and their wives and Mark were left. Obioha led the way as they ushered Mark into his new house.

"Mark, this is your house. I hope you will feel at home here, my brother." Obioha smiled broadly as he spoke.

Everyone turned to Mark to hear what he would say.

"Thank you, my family," he said, hugging everyone. "I'm sure I will be happy here."

"You will eat with us until a houseboy is employed to prepare your food. The nurse we arranged for you will start work tomorrow. Welcome home, my brother." Obioha embraced Mark and held him close for a few seconds.

***

The first thing that struck Mark in Umuokpa was that there was no electricity. When he asked, he was told that power supply ceased over a year ago. The rural electrification scheme collapsed, so Umuokpa had not had electricity for more than a year. In the absence of electricity supply from the national grid, the well-to-do in Umuokpa resorted to using power generating sets. There was too much noise from the numerous generators. Mark found it insufferable. The house behind Mark's bungalow, which belonged to one of their relations, had its generating set roaring away all night and almost all day. *Kpakpururu ... Kpakpurururu ... Kpukpu ... Kpukpu.* A short distance away, a different kind of sound was heard. *Gbidigbidi ... gbidigbidi ... vuuuu ... vuuuu ... vuvuvuvuu.* Mark was so distressed that he began to interprete the language of the generator to himself. He thought the generator was asking him: *Onye ije, ebee ka isi* – meaning Stranger, where are you from? The thought frightened him. Even Obioha's generator did not spare him. It roared all night and sometimes in the day time. The smell of the fumes was unbearable. It made Mark sneeze most of the time. His head ached and ached. He could not sleep well at night.

"What is happening? Don't these generators ever stop?" Mark asked Adaoma, the nurse.

"Sir, this is what we go through in Umuokpa. We do not have electricity so everyone uses generators; even the poor resort to the toyish ones that make the worst kind of noise. My neighbor's generator drives me crazy sometimes. The sound goes up, descends and goes up again. Then it fires like gunshots: *Kpakpakpa kpaaaaa! Kpakpakpa kpaaaaa! Kpaaaaa!* It annoys me, but sometimes I find it entertaining and laugh and laugh."

"I can't bear this!" Mark cried. "It's too much!"
Adaoma shrugged. "You'll get used to it, sir."

Before the month ended, Mark had run out of patience. Something drastic had to be done, he thought. He was beginning to question the wisdom of relocating to Nigeria. It didn't seem he could survive in the new enviroment in which he found himself. Lagos was unsuitable. And now Umuokpa did not seem to be any better. Moreover, he didn't like the way the extended family visited early in the morning to greet him. Six o'clock in the morning, when he was still asleep, they came to knock on the door. "Mmadu onokwa ebea? Is there no one in this place?" And they would not stop knocking or calling out until someone answered the door. What would he do now? The idea of the nursing home in Edinburgh did not seem so bad anymore.

Mark was in this state of indecision when Umuokpa was attacked by marauding herdsmen weilding dangerous weapons, especially those called AK47. Some weeks ago, some farmers and herdsmen had clashed because the herdsmen led their cattle into extensive farmlands and destroyed crops. No one knew where the attackers came from or how they got to Umuokpa, but by the time they had finished with the village several houses had been razed and many men, women and children slaughtered like animals. Fortunately, Obioha, his family and Mark escaped the deadly attack.

One week after, Mark went to see Obioha. "My brother, I cannot stay in Umuokpa after this madness. What kind of country is this? People were killed like animals and nothing came out of it. No one has been arrested. The perpetrators have not been arrested or punished. And when the victims tried to fight back and defend themselves, the police told them not to take the law into their own hands and threatened to arrest them." Mark was fuming.

"It is shocking and abominable," agreed Obioha. "The State Governor made a broadcast. He said something would be done. We are waiting."

"I can't take this. I don't want to die in the hands of heartless and mindless killers. I have decided to return to

Edinburgh. I'm sorry, if I disappoint you, but my mind is made up. I'll contact my son tomorrow."

***

Mark returned to Lagos on an evening flight a few days later. Chiedozie and the driver met him at the domestic wing of the Murtala Mohammed Airport.

"Your call-up letter for the National Youth Service has not been issued yet?" Mark asked Chidozie as they drove out of the airport car park.

"No, Uncle. They asked us to check for it on campus next week."

It was a Sunday, so traffic was not very heavy. They got to Lekki much faster than the other time.

Having made up his mind to return to Edinburgh, Mark began to look forward to it as days rolled by. The nightmarish experience at Umuokpa haunted him. With Chidozie's assistance, he packed his suitcase and bought a few things he needed. Onumba booked a flight for him and came over to the Guest Chalet on the eve of Mark's departure.

"Mark, I am really so sorry that you decided to return to the United Kingdom. However, you are welcome in case you change your mind now or in the future." He sat in the very chair he sat the day Mark had told him he wanted to live in Umuokpa. The only thing missing was his loud laughter. Both brothers were in a sombre mood.

"I'm sorry things turned out this way, but I think I am a misfit in this country; I stayed away too long and now I know I don't belong here. Please forgive me for all the trouble you went through to welcome me and make me comfortable. You, Mma, Obioha and Ugoma." Mark's voice trailed off. He did not know what else to say.

"That's okay. It was no trouble at all. Though it didn't work out, I'm glad you were home for a while." Onumba got up and walked to the door.

"Good night," Mark said softly.

"Good night. Ka chi fo," Onumba replied and shut the door.

The next day, at the Murtala Mohammed International Airport, the brothers bade each other goodbye. They knew they might not see each other again. If Mark entered the nursing home, it was not likely he would ever leave it alive. It was a prison of a sort for those who moved in there. There was also no sign that his children would ever ask him to move into their homes. They might visit him once in a while in the nursing home, but there he would remain till the end of his life. That much he knew. But he was ready. He accepted his fate.

As if on cue, both of them opened their arms and embraced. They held each other tight. Then they drew apart. "Goodbye, my brother. Safe trip." Onumba waved.

"Goodbye, Onumba," Mark said, waving too.

"Let's keep in touch," Onumba said firmly.

"Yes, we'll do that." Mark turned and walked slowly towards the attendant with a wheelchair, waiting for him.

Four

Out of Sight

CHISOM PARKED THE SUV AT THE BACK of the house and jumped out. Her handbag was sitting on the passenger seat and she climbed into the car again to get it. Her hand was unsteady as she tried to lock the car. At last she succeeded to insert the key in the hole and, turning it, she heard the lock click. She ran up the stairs and did not stop until she got to the second floor that she occupied with her family. Chisom knocked on the door and waited, her body vibrating from excitement. She glanced at her wrist watch. It was three o'clock in the afternoon. She knew her twin boys of five would be having their afternoon nap at that time, but was sure Dubem was somewhere in the flat. Wondering why he did not come to open the door, Chisom banged on it, waited a second and banged again. "Open the door for me," she yelled.

At last she heard movements inside and soon the door swung open to reveal an angry Dubem staring at her. "Why are you banging on the door like this, Chisom? Is something wrong?"

Without answering his question, Chisom rushed into the sitting room and flung her bag on the nearest chair. Then she turned to face her husband, who still stood at the door, looking at her as though she had gone crazy. "Honey, don't look at me like that. I have great news!" Before Dubem could react, Chisom threw her arms around his neck and laughed wildly.

Dubem shut the door with his left foot and, holding his wife around the waist, drew slightly away from her to be able to see her face. "Now, Chisom, tell me what this is all about. The boys are asleep; don't wake them up, please." He drew her to a seat and sat near her. "What's the news?"

Chisom tried to control herself. "Honey, I'm sorry if I acted like I'm crazy, but wait till you hear the news. I've been awarded the Fellowship! Yes, I've been awarded a Commonwealth Fellowship for six months and will spend it at the Institute of Education, University of London. A Visiting Commonwealth Fellow! Doesn't that sound great? London, here I come!" Chisom jumped up and began to dance round the tastefully furnished sitting room, weaving in between the upholstered chairs.

"That is good news, indeed!" Dubem beamed with pleasure. "Congratulations, darling! This calls for a celebration. Shall we eat out this evening? We'll go with the boys."

"Great! They'll love it," Chisom said, sitting down again on the chair she left some minutes ago. She leaned against Dubem and he circled her slim waist with his right hand. "So I won't have to prepare dinner tonight. In any case, I'm too excited to think of cooking at the moment."

Dubem smiled at her. "I share your excitement. It couldn't have been easy winning the Commonwealth Fellowship. It is very competitive."

"You're right," Chisom said, sitting up and gesticulating with both hands. "You know, I learned that there were over a hundred applications in our discipline and only five of us were selected for the award."

"My brilliant wife, I salute you." Dubem beamed at her proudly.

The idea that she was one of the lucky few that won the Fellowship Awards triggered Chisom's excitement once more. She got up again and began to sing and dance at the same time.

> Gini ka m ga-eji kele Chineke?
> Gini ka m ga-eji kele onye kere ụwa?
> Gini ka m ga-eji kele Ọkaka?
> Na ngozi nile ọ goziri mụ n'elu ụwa.
> [What shall I render to you my God?
> What shall I render to the Creator of the world?
> What shall I render to Almighty God?
> For all the blessings he bestowed on me.]

Dubem followed her movements with his eyes. Chisom had always been emotional, he thought, but this time there was a good reason for it. He was thinking of which restaurant to take his family to, when the sound of a door shutting loudly startled him. But, as he was getting up, two energetic little boys burst into the sitting room. Chudi and Chika, the identical twins! It was not always easy for Dubem and Chisom to tell the twins apart.

"Mummy, why are you singing and dancing?" the twins asked together. "We heard you from our room," Chudi added. They stared at their mother, who continued to sing and dance happily.

It was Dubem who answered them. "Your mummy has something to celebrate and we'll celebrate with her. Later this evening, we'll go to Amigo Restaurant for dinner."

"Wow! Thank you, Daddy!" Chudi shouted and Chika echoed him.

The next few months were occupied with marking examination scripts and preparing results, and securing travelling documents. Armed with a letter from the Commonwealth Office in London and one from the University of Lagos, her employer, it was easy for Chisom to get a visa from the British High Commission in Lagos. Her widowed mother agreed to move into her house to take care of the twins and their father while she was away. At first Dubem said he could manage, but he was delighted when his mother-in-law was finally installed in the guest room in their three-bedroom flat, a week before Chisom departed for London.

"Honey, take care of yourself and the twins and my mother too," Chisom said, anxiety written all over her beautiful face. She looked attractive in her pink housecoat.

"You don't need to worry, darling," Dubem said. "We'll be fine. Take care of yourself. And remember that you have a husband waiting for you. Remember you're my wife." He gave her a meaningful look before turning to put the television on for the evening news.

Chisom stared at him. "What do you mean? Of course, I know I'm your wife and you are my husband." His remark upset her. She was conscious of the fact that this was the first time they were going to be separated from each other for longer than a few days. Until this time, they had always been together and when any of them travelled for longer than a week, they travelled together. His job hardly took him out of Lagos and on the few occasions he travelled alone, it was never for more than a few days. "You'll see. I'll be back before you miss me. As for me, I'll be so busy that I won't have time to think of anything outside my work except, perhaps, you and the twins."

Dubem turned to look at her and smiled. As he hugged her, he whispered, "I'm glad you said that."

***

It was difficult at first to find a good, comfortable and affordable accommodation in London. Chisom did not want to spend all the money she received on accommodation. Initially, she spent a few days in a hotel in Central London but found it too expensive. She moved to a house in Brixton owned by a Nigerian and occupied by some Nigerian students, but it was too cold and damp. Hot water was not regular. She was in this dilemma when the Head of the Department to which she was attached assisted her in getting a suitable accommodation in one of the University of London halls of residence reserved for graduate students. With her new residence, Chisom thought she was set to work hard, churn out well-researched papers and give the two seminar papers she owed the Department as part of the condition for her stay. She was also assigned an hour or two of teaching at the Master's level.

It was October and Chisom had not reckoned with the inclement British winter that was at London's doorstep. She was shocked how cold the weather could get and was informed that it would get colder between December and February. "I hope I will not die of cold in this city," she murmured each time the weather got colder. The only time she felt warm was when she was in the College library. So she stayed long in the library every day, except at the weekend. Her room was not as warm as the library, except when she was under the blankets.

"Wanja, you said you've been in this country for a year?" Chisom asked her next-door neighbor, a Kenyan from the University of Nairobi. "Tell me, how does one deal with this cold? I'm cold most of the time. It's a nightmare for me having come from a hot country." Both of them had been reading in the library and came out for a few minutes to buy snacks before returning to their work. Chisom pulled her jacket closer and buttoned it up to her neck. Her fingers were cold and pale in spite of her fair skin. Her legs were beginning to peel and release some fluffy and whitish dead skin.

Wanja laughed and placed her left hand on Chisom's lap. They sat on a long chair made from concrete in the garden near the library. "Chisom, don't worry, you'll manage. Winter is winter and will be cold, but we fight it with warm clothes, heat and hot tea. And you could find yourself a boyfriend, you know." Wanja laughed again, her eyes teasing. Her narrow face was friendly and full of mirth.

"A boyfriend!?" Chisom was horrified. "Didn't I tell you I am married and have two children?"

"But, you asked me how you could fight the cold. What better way can you have warmth than being close to a human body?" Wanja was still laughing. Sensing that Chisom did not like the joke, she added quickly, "On a more serious note, you need to have a better heating device in your room. The central heating in the building has not been activated. It comes fully in late October or early November, I think."

"But this is October," Chisom said. "I hope they won't wait until I'm dead before activating it." She gazed around her and marveled at the intimidating buildings surrounding the Institute. London is awesome in its brutal beauty, she thought. She was thinking: *You are on your own; you do your own thing in your own way here; no one cares. However, the day you commit a crime is the day you feel the long arm of the law reaching out for you.*

Chisom shivered as if from cold and fear. She was grateful for Wanja's friendship.

"When we get back to our rooms, I'll show you how to increase the heat in the room. London is cold, but not as cold as some towns in the north. What would you have done if you had to spend your fellowship year in Edinburgh, for example? It's cold and windy there."

"I would simply go back to my country," Chisom said quickly. She had forgotten how she sang and danced around when she received the letter informing her of the fellowship award.

"You must be joking," Wanja reprimanded her with mock severity. "Do you know how many people would give up something valuable to be where you are today? I tell you, you'll get used to the cold. You'll manage."

They finished their snacks, drank their tea and returned to the library.

Chisom and Wanja left the library just before ten o'clock when it closed for the day. When they got to Leicester Hall, they separated and Chisom went up to her room. She dropped her books on her reading table and placed her handbag on one of the chairs. She had a quick bath and decided to go to bed right away. She was tired, having worked in the library almost the whole day. Besides, she felt a little sad; she missed her family. The previous night she had dreamed of Dubem, and the dream was about their early days after they met at a youth convention. It had been love at first sight and their friends teased them, for they were always seen together everywhere. That was eight years ago. How time flew, she thought.

Chisom changed into her night dress and lay in bed, facing the ceiling in the darkened room. She had drawn the curtain to ward off the light that shone in from the electric pole outside her window. It amazed her that there was never power outage in London, at least since she arrived. It was not so in Lagos, where there was constant power outage. She shut her eyes and her mind turned to Dubem, who was a pupil engineer at a construction company when they met. She was an assistant lecturer in the University of Lagos and was in a doctoral program in the university at the time. They got married two years after meeting. Remembering all this, Chisom smiled. Dubem was dark-skinned and handsome. When he was courting her, just the sight of him made her go all weak. She sighed heavily.

Sleep seemed to be far from her. Chisom turned and faced the wall. Her arms ached to hold Dubem. Her heart ached from missing him. She longed to love him physically. To have and to hold as they vowed the day they got married in church! Seeing young men and women holding hands and kissing in the streets of London or in the trains reminded her of her loneliness. She missed Dubem and the twins terribly. In the midst of these thoughts she drifted into sleep.

Three weeks after, a Ghanaian lecturer in one of the Colleges of the University of London invited friends and colleagues to his birthday party and asked them to bring along their friends. Wanja was a friend of the lecturer and invited Chisom to the party. The birthday party took place in a community hall in Hackney. Chisom was to discover that many Ghanaians and Nigerians lived in that part of London. When they arrived, they were welcomed by booming African music. Chisom felt her spirit lift as she witnessed the convivial atmosphere. Most of the guests were black. Some people were already dancing. Wanja was immediately engaged in a dance by a young man she told Chisom was her boyfriend. Chisom found herself swaying to the rhythm of the pulsating music. A tall and good-looking man came over and asked her to dance with him. She hesitated and was at the point of rejecting the offer, when the man spoke.

"Come on, you can't sit here and just watch the band performing. I'm Clifford from Ghana; you can call me Cliff. What's your name?"

"I'm Chisom, from Nigeria."

Chisom, let's go and dance." And when she said nothing and still sat down, he added, "Please, don't say no. These lovely legs are made for dancing." He was looking at her legs.

Chisom laughed, wondering how he knew that she had lovely legs, for her legs were not showing. She allowed him to lead her to the busy dance floor. The celebrant was dancing with a woman who was probably his wife. He held her close and they moved elegantly on the floor. Chisom and Clifford began to dance. He was more or less her dancing partner that evening. He hardly danced with any other woman and she too did not dance with any other man.

Around eight o'clock, Chisom noticed that people were beginning to leave. She looked round and saw that Wanja had disappeared with her boyfriend. Chisom almost panicked as she was not sure she would be able to find her way back to Leicester Hall from where she was. How could Wanja leave without even bothering to tell her? She frowned.

"My friend who invited me to the party has gone," Chisom confided in Clifford. "I hope I can find my way to my place."

"Don't worry. I can take you to any part of London," Clifford reassured her. "Where do you live?"

"I live in Central London, in Leicester Hall."

"That's not a problem. I know the place and will take you there. Relax."

"Thank you, but I'll like to go now. If you want to stay longer, I can ask other guests for the bus or train route. I usually use Piccadilly Line and get out at Euston Station, which is close to my place. I could also get down at King's Cross Station, which is just a short distance away."

"We can go now," Clifford said. "Just a minute, I'll get my jacket."

Chisom was pleased to have his company. He was quite friendly and danced well. The train station was near and in a few minutes they were on their way. He sat opposite Chisom and each time she looked up, she found him staring at her. If their eyes met, he smiled and she decided not to look at him. After four stops, Clifford got up and asked her to follow him. She stood up quickly and followed him before the doors closed.

"Is this Euston Station? I don't recognize it."

"No. This is my stop; my house is nearby and I need to pick up something before taking you to Euston. It's a parcel for my sister who lives in South East London. My house is not far from here, so you don't need to worry."

Chisom thought about it and decided to follow him. A few minutes delay would do no harm, she thought. When they got to his door, she said, "I'll wait for you here. Please hurry; it's getting late."

"Why wait in the cold, Chisom? Are you afraid of me?" Clifford laughed. "Come in with me; it won't take long to pick up the stuff. Besides there is no harm in knowing my place, in case you ever want to get in touch after today."

That too sounded quite reasonable and Chisom stepped into the room after him. He showed her a chair in the sitting room and then walked into an inner room. Chisom studied the room. The three chairs in the room were old, but clean. There was a gas heater by the corner and an old cupboard. A framed picture of Clifford hung on the wall and Chisom admired it. He was truly a good-looking man, she thought. He was dressed in a traditional outfit made from Kente material. She looked at her watch and saw that it was past nine o'clock. "Hello, Cliff! What's keeping you? I must leave now."

Clifford came out dressed differently and walked directly to where Chisom sat on the edge of the chair. He pulled her up gently and pressed her against his body. "Chisom you're so beautiful. I've fallen for you, you know. Let's have some fun before I take you home."

Chisom glared at him and tried to push him away. He held her firmly and, freeing his right hand, he began to stroke her back. She was frightened. "No, you can't do this," she cried. "Let me go." The image of Dubem flashed across her mind and she struggled harder to free herself.

Clifford fumbled with her clothes in an attempt to undress her, starting with the jacket that he tried to remove. He was breathing heavily and begging her to cooperate. The thought of Dubem armed Chisom with strength. She gave Clifford a sudden and violent push that sent him sprawling. She ran forward and, pulling the door open, escaped into the night. She did not stop running until she reached the train station. Chisom only looked back once to see if Clifford was following her. She did not care if she missed her way; all she wanted was to be far from him and never to set eyes on him again.

As soon as she got into the train, she looked at the drawing that marked out the different stations on the Piccadilly Line and was relieved that Euston was only a few stops from where she was.

As the train jolted away, Chisom closed her eyes, thinking of Dubem and of her narrow escape.

Omofolabo Ajayi-Soyinka

Omofolabo Ajayi-Soyinka, Ph.D., interdisciplinary scholar, creative artist, feminist activist, performer, choreographer, and mother, had joint appointments in the Theatre Department and Women's, Gender and Sexuality Studies (WGSS) Department, University of Kansas (KU) Lawrence, U.S.A., until her 2015 retirement after twenty-five years as Professor Emerita. Dr. Ajayi-Soyinka continues to publish as an Independent Scholar, and remains engaged in civic activism. She had taught in the Department of Dramatic Arts, Obafemi Awolowo University (formerly University of Ife), Nigeria, and was detained under Ibrahim Babangida regime for her academic and civic activism. Ajayi-Soyinka later left Nigerian for Cornell University, Ithaca, U.S.A. with a Post-Doctoral Fellowship award. Dr. Ajayi-Soyinka's teaching, research publications, and creative works encompass the rich fields of theatre, literature, race, and gender studies, including the critical theories that inform them. In addition to book chapters, Encyclopedia entries, and articles in scholarly journals, Dr. Ajayi-Soyinka is the author of *Yoruba Dance* (1998), co-editor of *African Literature at the Millennium* (2006), and *Reflections: An Anthology of New Works by African Women Poets* (2013), and in between experiments with the writing of poetry and short stories. Performed and choreographed works include *Death and the King's Horseman* (Wole Soyinka; Kalamazoo College, 2008). *Oyedipo at Kolhuni* (Wole Soyinka; Delphi, Greece, 2002), and *Many Colours Make the Thunder King* (Femi Osofisan, Gutherie, too! Minnesota, 1997). Professor Ajayi-Soyinka is an active member of several organizations, President of the African Literature Association (2009-2010), and member of the Executive Council of African Studies Association, Association of African Women Scholars (AAWS), and Lawrence Arts Council, Kansas. Inducted into the Women's Hall of Fame at Kansas University (KU), Ajayi-Soyinka was also a Fulbright Scholar (2008), the recipient of the Glidden Visiting Professorship, Ohio University, Athens, OH, and the Kansas Humanities Council (KHC) "ROADS" Scholar, among others.

Five

Resident Alien

MY DEAR BIM-BIM,

THANK YOU SO MUCH for not throwing this letter away with the envelope. Unopened. I would not have blamed you, if you had. I, too, would have. However, I could never match the eloquence of your original, impromptu and out-of-this-world curses and abuses as you reported me to our friends at Club Freedom 77. Only this time, you would mean every sense of all you say, and it would be no laughing matter. But, since you have gotten this far, I implore you to keep on reading. And bear with me, as I share with you what my eyes have seen. Let me quickly add that I am grateful to God for having gotten this far, at all.

Forgive my long silence. It was never my intention to cut off my friends, you especially. I know it will look like now that I have legally made it to America, complete with the famed Green Card, I have forgotten my friends. No! No! No! Bee, things have been quite difficult. I mean DIFFICULT. Not just 'difficult' as a figure of speech, or as an excuse for not getting in touch with you since I left home .... Was that not three years ago? How time flies, or drags, I no longer know; perception has been altered for me. The dreams I had, that we all had. "America, here I come!" Oh, the promises I made. I have not forgotten my promise to send for you and Dee-dee within a year of coming here. There was no question I would "have made it" by then. Dreams, hah!

"Made it, within a year!" What a delusionary dream! We all want our dreams to come true, if only what we dream is reality. But we cannot but hope, for it is hope that gets us closer to making those dreams real, as real as we want them. If only everybody's reality is our own individual reality. Or, if only we knew of everybody's reality while we were dreaming our own dreams, so we could adjust how our dreams would transform into reality as we travel on the wings of hope towards our aspirations. So, let me dream on, and pray that I will "have made it" by the time I turn 80.

Would you believe it? I earned my first pay just two months ago. It was $20.00 payment for a three-hour job washing dishes at a restaurant. My roommate said it was a very generous pay, given that I had no work experience, and my accent.... My accent! No work experience! Generous pay! I am sure you will be outraged with me. That is only the tip of the iceberg, and it is about the gentlest chiding to that kind of reaction. Usually, I have a curt "face the facts, babe" flung at my direction.

A few months back, I would have flown off the handle and given the young woman a good lecture about my 20-year work experience, my Master's degree in child psychology and social welfare and the 35-person-staff department I headed back home. What am I talking about!? Just six months ago, I ranted, raved and, yes, wallowed in self-righteous pity at Tanto, an old school-mate of ours back in elementary school. Nondescript, she was. I don't think you will remember her. But, I was desperate enough to gamble it would be her, when I read that unusual first name, "Tantolorun" in the phonebook. She tolerated me for almost 18 months before throwing me out of her apartment. Anyway, she suggested that I go to work at MacDonald's, just to keep body and soul together, while I waited to get a job more befitting of my status. I don't know which incensed me more; her hardly disguised sarcasm or what I thought was an arrogant "I've-made-it-why-can't-you?" attitude. Now, I know better. Last month, I began working at Sonic's Drive-In, where I have to serve customers in their cars.

Do you know what that means? I, who could barely survive our Harmattan season of 50 degrees at its coldest and with the sun shining merrily. Now, I am out there in the snow, and not a ray of the sun to behold. I am hopping from car to car, a tray of fries and coffee balanced in my hands and the temperature is -3 degrees. After only two trips, walking becomes laborious. My face is congealed, my toes are frozen and my hands completely numb. I am so clumsy that I am not able to pick up the change called 'tips' that they throw at me disgustedly from the snow where it had fallen. Do you blame them? I am constantly wiping my dripping nose with the back of my hand. I asked to be transferred where customers place orders. They did, but I cannot understand their accents. You know, Americans have accent, too! Everything is nasalized, a twang or a drawl. Now, put that through the ordering microphone, and you are in big trouble. Everything comes out so muffled that I cannot understand a thing. I mix up orders. You can't imagine how bad! So, they transfer me to the frying section. After I pass out twice from the heat, I am back to the car-hopping beat.

Laura, my roommate can't believe I can't take the heat in the kitchen. She said she'd seen Africans on CNN cooking for whole villages under huge open fires in open spaces, the sun blazing away and she never saw anybody pass out. She was graceful enough to add that I probably had a "hovel kitchen," since my English is not too bad. Still, she thinks African kitchen heat is just as intense as the heat of the tropical sun. I smile; I take it as a compliment. Now you stop that colorful stream of name-calling and curses. And don't you dare mention it at Freedom 77! I know. That's what I am reduced to. But take it from me, it take it as a compliment, having heard worse. And Laura is a sweet girl, naïve, young, but well-meaning. She's been a ton of help too.

In any case, I am already dreading the summer time, when we have to roller skate for our car hops. I hope by then, I would have gotten another job. My first roller skating lesson ended in disaster. Can you imagine me with broken hips at my age and no health insurance? Permanent case of split personality - hips one direction, head the other. The welfare system has been so radically "reformed" that only big Corporations benefit from it. Forget Worker's Compensation or Social Security. I don't have enough work equity. Tanto said the Social Security people recently informed her she needs ten more working years before she can qualify for any Social Security benefits. This is after working for 12 years, six of them within a very plushy income bracket. I need a long hope.

I am sure you are wondering about my Green Card, the magical green card that would put the American Dream immediately within my laps. I too asked myself the same question for three years. Or, you think I have gone completely off my rockers? No way! That is your uncontested privilege, remember? I am the sane one of all Freedom 77 members. Besides, unless you are a super millionaire, America has no time for eccentrics like you. You'd be surprised. For three years, I was berating this country, demanding to know why it asked me to come if unwilling to give me a job. Not any job, but the type of job I deserve by my qualification, experience and willingness. Before I was given the Green Card, they read my application form. I listed all my certificates, credentials and job experience and letters of references from who is who in the profession. For three years, I was carrying my real, well, what I thought was my real C.V., from office to office, from employer to employer, and believing my qualifications would be my most eloquent advocates. Look, I am not getting paranoid, but I believe I got more letters of rejections than the total number of applications I sent out. Yet, if I am to believe Tanto, and I am beginning to believe everything Tanto ever told me, for every letter of rejection I got, five of my application letters ended in the garbage can (that is dust bin in American Speak, if you don't know), unopened. Apparently, the Golden Rule here is "you get what you negotiate, not what you deserve."

Okay! The next stage - going to offices to fill job forms. By this time, I had scaled down my expectation a little bit and did not expect my letters to speak for me well enough. I was ready to negotiate. I thought, if they saw me, heard me, saw samples of my work, I would surely get a job. Big mistake! Have you seen me lately? Two years of stress, worry, anger, hunger and frustration have all eaten into my face, skin and posture. They not only wanted fresh graduates, they wanted young women. Here I was, 45, looking like my mother at 75. I didn't blame them.

It turned out that my biggest hurdle was computer knowledge, not the art of negotiation. Computer? They were not invented while and where I was going to school. Our much touted "transfer of technology" back home was to trade money from the agricultural exports for importation of foreign Oil Companies to drill oil and destroy our farmlands. So "transfer of technology" failed to translate into investment in computer technology. Q. E. D. By the time we finally got a computer in my department, there were too many demands on it and not one computer-literate person; it broke down in no time. In this country, every school child has access to a computer. I am NOT exaggerating, it's too painful. One woman actually stopped me halfway through the form and told me not to bother completing it. She noticed I had marked "none" in the box for computer experience.

Must everything depend on computer? I am not anti-computer, but what about people? People know things, people do things, people talk to people, deal with children. Heck, I am a trained child psychologist with 20 years of experience. I know how to prepare budgets for departments. I know how to run departments, run workshops, organize conferences, and arrange meetings. I manage offices and I know the filling system. I can be a receptionist, clerk, I don't mind even if I have to do files! Oh, Lord. I don't believe I just said that. Shows how much I have come down... No! Tanto said I must not think like that. So, rather let me say, it shows how much I have learnt to appreciate the Green Card. This is getting really depressing. I need some music.

Hi, Bee, it's me again since yesterday. I put on our favorite Fela Anikulapo music, "Kalakuta Republic." I danced all evening, and then went to see a movie. Kalakuta Republic, indeed! Such craziness, and he thought our inept, bloated government would allow him to get away with it. But, he so beautifully captured and epitomized the spirit of defiance and independence of our times. We should have made him an honorary member of freedom 77. Put a Fela on, will you? Let's relive this brief moment of euphoria together across the gulf of collapsed dreams. Oh, how I laughed when I remembered all the good times and impromptu parties we used to have. Heaven knows what our children must have thought of our Club, but they had fun, too. And thank goodness, see how well they have turned out. If only our leaders had turned out half as well.

Laura came in, while I was jiving down memory lane of better times and almost passed out. She said she was beginning to think I was not really African. Africans are supposed to be happy-go-lucky people, always full of laughter and not a worry in the world. They are such great dancers, too, but I had always been sad, gloomy and moody. I asked her if her favorite Africans from the T.V.-world of refugee camps and begging bowls were laughing and dancing. Yes, I was back to my old self. Briefly. My voice must have been so cutting and bitter that she began to apologize profusely. The movie was her idea, her way of making amends. Of course, I paid my way! No, I did not pay for her, she invited me. This is America! No age deference. When I invite her, I may pay, and that's only if it does not make her feel beholden to me.

I was talking about computer terrorism before I took a break yesterday. Bee, I tell you, I am readier than ever to learn that damn computer. But, where is the time, where is the money? I work 10 hours a day, 6 days, and sometimes 7 days a week. At the end of each day, I am a wreck, physically and emotionally. I numb my mind, so I don't think and risk going crazy. Computer costs money and I can't pay my rents. I am ashamed to say, but I AM IN DEBT! I have drawn so much on my credit card. I have overspent whatever interests would have accumulated when my bank Certificate of Deposit finally matures. That was Tanto's doing. She advised me to deposit the money I brought from home in a Certificate of Deposit and then borrow against it. Later, I could use one of those hundreds of credit card checks they keep sending me to pay off the bank. That way, I will have credit in two places - the bank and the credit card company.

Puzzled? Confused? Welcome to the Club. But it seems to be working. Pure magic! Worked like a charm! The very companies that had turned down my credit card application two years ago for having no credit history, now bombard me with pre-approved credit cards up to $100,000! Here in America, credit actually means debit. You get debt-ridden to be credit worthy. And the credit bestows on you a brand new identity. In addition to my new-found wealth, I also have a new name, Resident Alien, courtesy of the Green Card, of course, but a perfect complement to my credit-card carrying membership and identity.

In case you are too slow to get what I have been trying to tell you, perspectives are radically altered once you step off the plane at JFK Airport. Your sunny smiling Naija personality becomes a Resident Alien. Debit becomes credit. And you are thrown with your own debited credit self into a new exclusive identity. Plus, you are rich, paper rich. Bottom line, you get what you negotiate, not what you deserve. Only I am no longer certain what I negotiated and when or whether I deserve it or not. I simply shake my head; I have given up trying to understand the rationale. I can assure you, I am not anxious to add insanity to my new-found poverty status. I move with the flow, and I tell you I am learning fast. I even came up with a slogan. You will be so proud of me. "Get rich by credit cards! Your bankruptcy is guaranteed!" Now, I revel in the fact that I am rich and a mere signature away from $100,000. I am a rich woman car hopping French fries and hot coffee, in order to keep starvation and homelessness at bay. And we thought Nigeria was the ultimate in contradictions!

People tell me, I ain't seen nothing yet. Is that Nigerian or American? I am getting all my idioms mixed up. Anyway, I believe I have got you all so completely mixed up that you will not only pardon me, you will absolve me of all my iniquities.

Love to your children. Well, they are young adults now. And to our gang of "Freedom 77."

I sign off with all my titles.

Your
Debit-Rich, Sonic-Car-Hopping, Resident Alien
Mee F-77

Six

Peas a' Pod

MIGRATION, OR IF YOU LIKE, EXILE, IS a leveler. It cuts you down to size. A size so totally unrecognizable, even to you, that you wonder what happened to the rest of you. It is unsettling, it is destabilizing, but it is important to recognize, accept, and adjust to the dissociating effects of an immigrant status, in order to prevent even more catastrophic effects, especially for the second generation of immigrants. It is not an easy process, I can tell you, and particularly for those who have been endowed with an inflated, oversized sense of self-importance, merited or not, in their countries of origin, the reduction in size can truly make you develop serious mental problems. So, if only for sanity's sake, it helps to have a moderate opinion of one's self. Often, immigration happens unexpectedly, and if it gives any warning, chances are it is ignored. Life grinds on, oiled by hope.

Who in Nigeria was thinking of immigration in the early 1980s? The future looked promising, even the military dictators had settled into power and thought they had successfully cowed the population into obedience and/or sycophancy. Home was okay, there was oil boom. Then, bam! The bottom fell out; the military dictators got morbidly overbearing and the simmering discontent blew the lid off. Chaos does not mix well with desperation fueled by deprivation. Tell me who does not think of migrating these days out of her country, his homeland; from all over Africa, this ancient continent that for the past three decades has been steadfastly running backwards? Too many Africans, men, women, young, old, regardless of education, profession, or socio-economic status, are literally dying to get out of their environment, and abandon the little gems that give huge meaning to their very being. They are willing to mortgage their lives, and sometimes a whole generation's, paying top currency just to get out of their country. By top currency, I do not mean the type you load into a mini-van, because you want to buy a loaf of bread. I mean top currencies like the pound sterling and dollar; currencies whose largest denomination do not exceed one hundred, and are seldom in general circulation. That is the kind of country where most migrating Africans want to be now; a place that reminds them of how things used to be when they were children and looked forward to becoming responsible, valued citizens of a stable country. Alas, such expectations have since taken flight from their land, and now they too are in hot pursuit to capture their disappearing dreams wherever they land. Without hesitation, and at the slightest opportunity, they abandon - who, what, and where - all that converged to give them their identity. They swap their familiar environment, where they are cherished, loved, and even celebrated, for an alien space where, for all the promises it holds, their difference still defines them, and their foreignness is perceived as threatening and suspicious. With grim resolve, hopeful immigrants put their lives and trust in the hands of shifty, no-conscience, global human trafficker, and set off into a world-wide trip to perceived prosperity or possible death. Anything is better than the hopelessness routinely bequeathed unto them by their rulers' mindless greed.

Libya has become the popular gateway for many immigrants from West African countries. Under the care of reckless smugglers with little regard for human lives, migrants travel across the sweeping isolated Sahara desert, past hungry and corrupt border police, and the brutal scorching desert heat. Many die of thirst and hunger; the desert is strewn with corpses in varying degrees of decomposition, and bleached human bones stick out of the sand dunes. When they finally make it to Libya where the passage should be easier and faster, the next phase of travails awaits them in the thriving human market and illegal prisons that are the sources of forced labor for establishments in the country. The hapless immigrants are subjected to another form of extortion and torture, both physically and mentally. Apparently, or so they are informed, their "travel agents," the middlemen between the migrants and smugglers incorporated, have duped the migrants and failed to pay the Libyan smugglers their full due. And unless the captive human cargo pays up, they will be abandoned. The new levy can be up to two thousand dollars ($2,000.00). Only a few have the resources or dedicated relatives back home to raise the unexpected exorbitant amount. Even then, it takes months to get the transaction through. While waiting, they are infected with diseases, sodomized, raped, and subjected to torture, and forced labor. Some women get pregnant and are further burdened with unplanned babies. Many do not survive. For the majority unable to meet the new financial demands, it is a death sentence by years of slow, sadistic torture.

Eventually, the pack of emaciated migrants travels across Libya to Sabratha, a coastal town in northern Libya, for their last leg of the journey *en route* to Europe. Only a pitiful percentage of those who set out together from a particular donor country make it to the coast. But, being by the sea lifts their spirits and makes them think of the West African myth of Mami Water, that seductive, but deadly sea creature with a female human upper body and fish scales for the rest. Anyone, who gets hold of her comb or mirror when she swims ashore and can negotiate smartly before returning her property, is assured untold wealth. On the contrary, a poor negotiation skill is tantamount to a life sentence of misery. In Sabratha, the land of their dreams is clearly visible across the waters, and all they have to do is get into the boat, cross the Mediterranean Sea, and be smart once in Italy. Inside a 30-person maximum capacity boat, 100 people stuff themselves, and are willing to squeeze in a few dozens more. They know they are all in the same boat; the solidarity of desperate immigrants who have survived this far.

A 1st class engineering graduate with six years of experience in joblessness that enabled him to perfect the craft of letter-writing-job-applications is tightly hedged in-between the illiterate Baba Gardener, the victim of mindless boys' pranks at his High School. Impatiently demanding that he remove his sore-infected leg is the motor-park tout who, six years ago, would have addressed him smartly as "Oga, sir," with the hope of getting hired as a driver either at a cutting-edge Engineering company or as his personal driver. At the other end of the boat, Madam Cash is struggling to keep from being crushed and suffocated by those who surge against her, when sea turbulence tilts the boat dangerously down her side. Madame Cash once ruled the adire (tie-dye) market of Lagos, but the thriving local textile market crashed when importation of any form of tie-dye colors was banned during the nation's Operation Local Products (OPL). Meanwhile, OPL flooded the market with cheap second-hand clothes popularly referred to as "bend-down" from Europe, and with shiploads of expensive Belgian lace. "The two levels of the society have to be adequately clothed," one OPL Official justified. Madame Cash was charged with spreading the rumors that the OPL official floated the textile company importing the second-hand clothing and the Belgian lace. She was promptly arrested and her shop looted. Normally, people so charged are never heard of again, but here she is. In this immigrant boat, nobody asks questions, energy is reserved for breathing and imagining the uncertainty of the life that awaits one on the other side of the waters. Hope is never in short supply.

Yes, migration is a leveler, and continues to be, even beyond surviving the hazards of the journey. Those jam packed in the boat are the lucky ones, at least for the moment. They have survived the trauma of the desert, the treachery of the smugglers syndicate, escaped death by torture in Libya, and now precariously *en route* to Italy. They must also survive turbulence of the waters, and make it safely to the Italian shores inside a rickety boat loaded with over 300 percent its capacity. Italy is only a stop gap, a transit space, but it is at its shores that they can seize the mythical Mami Water's precious comb.

However, when those able to swim ashore get there, instead of Mami Water desperately begging to have her comb back and promising a lifetime of luxury and wealth, many are begging for pennies alongside the roadsides. They become undocumented immigrants.

Now, not all immigrants have to go through this treacherous path. Not all become undocumented either. There is another group of immigrants who complete their journey in a matter of hours, by air, in relative comfort, and enter their host country legitimately, and remain there for as long as their visitor's visa lasts. Unfortunately, many become undocumented when, by choice or unexpected turn of events they overstay their visas, and regularization as a resident becomes problematic. Undocumented immigrants disappear underground, exist in the shadows, and hustle at anything and everything. Some even specialize in "graveyard shifts," patrolling graveyards for recently deceased people, so they can search for and sell their social security numbers to other desperate undocumented immigrants. Many work with forged, stolen, or bought papers, and even though they are working three jobs, they are barely able to make a living, because they dare not negotiate for even minimum wage, much less negotiate for wages commensurate with their qualification. Others attain residency by rushing into a costly marriage of convenience that is prone to extortion. But, some are lucky, and the marriage of convenience becomes the real thing.

Invariably, these immigrants are at the mercy of those who help them to survive, even in the shadows. Until recently, undocumented immigrants who keep low profile, stay out of trouble, and slug it out diligently at "do you want fries with that?" type of jobs, are able to survive, rise through the ranks, and live their dream. They have negotiated smartly with Mami Water.

Once upon a time, Africans in Europe or America were better known, and referred to as scholars, students, interns, travelers, visitors, vacationers, conference participants, and they could not wait to return to their home countries once their objectives were achieved. Sadly, only a few people now remember such a time ever existed. How fortunes have changed; now migration out of the beleaguered continent is a constant stream, and everybody is simply lumped together as 'African immigrants.' At first, the migration came in trickles, and transitioning to full-time jobs and residency was still possible. Some outstanding individuals in their field of expertise even had jobs waiting for them before they arrived in the land of dreams. However, when the trickle became a deluge, such opportunities or goodwill dried up, including for qualified professionals, and bona fide students.

Mercifully, the immigrant heroines of this story, Dollah and Bhully did not have to experience the perils of the Sahara Desert, the sadism of the slave traders, or the nightmares at sea. They came by air, armed with a visa that enabled them to disappear underground once it expired. Dollah and Bhully are twins, although they are not aware of it. In fact, they never met until well in their mid-forties. Yet, they were neither separated at birth nor adopted by different parents. At the same time, it will not be too far-fetched to say they shared the same womb – metaphorically speaking, that is. They came to the USA separately, at different times, and under different circumstances, but they both share the same status as undocumented immigrants, and they have perfected the art of hustling. They are charmers and will survive any condition no matter how dire. The first thing that strikes you about them is their appearance. My, oh my, do they know how to put it together! Such natty dressers! They mix and match colors, fabrics, textures, styles, and no matter what, the assemblage is impeccable! Only the chosen ones can get away with a medley like that. They are such delightful visual artists in motion. And, then, there is the carriage! It is a total package. The way the neck sits on the body, balances with ease on the shoulders, then tilts at an angle that screams 'dare you mess with me,' is mesmerizing! All this is further accentuated with the 'I don't give a damn' headwear pushed out sideways, at the forehead, or wound round to convey an air of innocent serenity, a vivid contrast to the sassy head-wear message. The peculiar turn of the head quickens your curiosity even more, as the eyes settle on you either imperiously, disdainfully, respectfully or teasingly; you can never know which will be bestowed on the audience at any particular time. But, hey, you better take it. Now, add the walk, "fun won tan ni, sir!" You cannot copy it; it is fully patented. What you see is a million-dollar-artistic bundle resplendent in motion. In reality, the whole visual assemblage – the body construct, material art and the mobile exhibit - is worth much less. A lot less, I dare say.

In physical stature, however, the two remind me of the twin brothers in my secondary school many years back. We called them the Heavily Brothers. One is built like a wrestler, heavy, all muscles, about 6'10" tall, and looks like a giant to us diminutives. In spite of his imposing and intimidating physique, he is surprisingly mild in manners, and is the good old boy of the school establishment. The other twin cannot have been more than 4' 8" in height, short and stocky; he is a rebel with a passionate cause in search of possible answers to 'Why should I be so short?" This always lands him into trouble with our school authorities. People always find it difficult to believe they are close relations, much less twins.

Bhully, one of our immigrant heroine twins, is a buxom dark beauty. Tall and proportionally built, her frontal endowment is complemented by a perfectly sculpted backside, comfortably balanced on two sturdy thighs. Her slightly oblong face, with the right-sized nose, is beautifully crafted, and her robust cheeks taper off nicely to focus attention on the perfect embodiment of the African mouth, two full, gorgeous, sensuous lips that complement those two eggs she has for eyes. Bhully loves her body as much as she loves her food, and she carries her weight proudly and with dignity. You see her, you see a go-getter, nothing stops her, and so you better watch out!

As for Dollah, she is a carbon copy of Esu, the mischievous trickster deity in the Yoruba religious pantheon that must have tempted Obatala with one keg of palm wine too many when he started molding her. Dollah is short. Worse, her upper half is disproportionate to her lower half. Meanwhile, her skin color is a patchwork of light brown with dark blotches that many assume is the result of an unsustainable use of bleaching cream, but no, that is her natural skin color. Her facial features seem to be engaged in a perpetual war with each other: two full irregular lips that jut out way off her long chin; a nose too small and that just seems wrong for her round face; now perhaps, if her cheeks were a bit fleshier.... No matter what, Dollah is not the one to worry about what she cannot help; she simply finds a way around it and makes it work in her favor. So, she accepts her body as she has been given, and actually flaunts it – otherwise why has she chosen a profession whose primary tool is the body – dance! It is a huge saving grace that she retains the African DNA of that special backyard, and does she know how to use it? Oh yes!

But, here, in their physical differences, end the similarities between the two sets of un-identical twins; the immigrant sisters and the Heavily Brothers. In temperament, unlike those male twins, Dollah and Bhully are peas in a pod; they are a mirror-image of each other, in behavior, mannerisms, and life-styles, at least as adults. It is uncanny, almost spooky, the way they reflect each other. Funny, their eerie alikeness recalls for me again, another set of real-life twins - the famous Lijadu Sis-ters.

The Lijadu Sisters delighted the young and old in the Nigeria of the mid-1960s to the late 1980s with their original rendition of folk songs. They had the same mannerisms, dressed alike all the time, were also noted for finishing each other's sentences, and outlined sequentially the same talking points on randomly chosen topics. They were totally identical and mischievously challenged people to creatively tell them apart. Like many others, the Lijadu Sisters too, had become blurry members of the African immigration statistics, but they had been able to maintain their art, and re-invent themselves to become productive members of their new homeland.

Even though they lack that natural mystery of actual identical twins, Dollah and Bhully seem to be drawn irresistibly to the same things, the same location and experience of similar problems. It is as if there exists an invisible communication system relaying messages between them across distances, gradually drawing them closer till they find themselves in Lilville, Podgate, where they finally meet face to-face, through Kita, also an exile and their reluctant mentor.

Kita is one of the lucky ones. She arrives in the US initially for a two-year exchange research program, but barely a month before her program ends, political violence erupts in her country, making it dangerous for her to return home. However, rather than opt for the usual political asylum, she applies for a visa extension facilitated by her colleagues, believing the situation will be back to normal within a year at the maximum. Then, the trickle begins, starting with her husband and children, bearing bad news that the situation back home is extensive, and has no immediate solution in sight. Kita and her husband start looking for permanent jobs and begin the transition to residency. That is some twenty-five years ago. Unlike other well-qualified professionals that arrive just a few years after her and the morphing of the trickle into a deluge, she escapes working at the minimum wage level or joining the army of growing undocumented immigrants. Rather, she is able to secure a job as a professional in her field, based on her educational qualification, and able to sustain her familiar middle-class status. Nonetheless, it is a struggle to adjust to her status as an immigrant; she must go through the mandatory Migration Educational System (MES), and earn a new degree, B.A. - Begin Again. The courses are numerous, varied, and constantly changing; it is a lifetime of learning, but after 25 years, Kita can claim she has earned some bold colors, except when dealing with Dollah and Bhully, our identical, un-identical twins of this story.

When her new job brings Kita to Littleville, Podgate, affectionately referred to as Lil' or Lil'Pod, by locals, a childhood friend from back home but now living in Lil' warns her.

"Do not get mixed up with those exiles."

She mutters her gratitude as expected, but she is annoyed. She fumes:

"Why does she think she has to warn me? And she referred to them as 'those exiles,' too. What kind of crap is that? As if she is not an exile herself! The arrogance!" she concludes self-righteously.

In no time, Kita becomes involved with her fellow exiles, a rag-tag collection of people with different educational and socio-economic backgrounds. Back in their homeland, they would be worlds apart, and their paths would probably never cross, having very little in common. By contrast, here, in their home away from home, they are all African immigrants, a status that disproportionately magnifies normal, routine daily problems. Kita's constant mantra is:

"We exiles have to stick together and minimize our problems. We are in a strange land, and we not only have to share, but also we have to be supportive of one another in our experiences of difference and otherness."

It does not matter whether they are documented or undocumented, she respects their work ethic and their determination to begin again and succeed. She recognizes that many are making honest living, sometimes working three different jobs so as not to live off the system. She admires them for the discipline.

"These are the type of people we need to restore the capabilities of our home country," she tells anybody who cares to listen, adding quietly to herself, "exile is a leveler, but it also promotes solidarity."

However, she soon discovers solidarity has boundaries. With her, the boundary is integrity wrapped around ideology, and there is no way politics cannot be in the mix, especially given the contributing factors to the collapse of their country. To her disappointment, she discovers her fellow immigrants will not touch politics with a ten-mile pole. At first, she attributes their reluctance to fear, and tries to convince them otherwise. But, anytime she attempts to discuss why it is important to be involved, and how the African Diaspora can unite to bring about positive changes in their homeland, conversations slow down and eventually peter out; she is nicknamed the 'party-pooper.' When she finds out that some of her solidarity friends are hustling for positions and contracts with the corrupt government back home, she limits her interaction to the few still with their integrity intact, and importantly, becomes more security conscious.

By the time Bhully comes to town, Kita's new placard of "solidarity with boundaries" has firmly supplanted the earlier 'solidarity forever' slogan. She still maintains cordial relations with her fellow Nigerian exiles, but she no longer wants to have any close dealings with them, ever again, much to the consternation, and confusion of her children, whom she has managed to turn into perfect bicultural children. They switch identities like you switch house lights on and off. She makes them understand that their Americanness stops as soon as they reach the entrance door to their home. Once inside, they are in Nigeria, and Nigerian rules and customs always apply. The smart children are quick to see a loophole, so whenever they are outside the house, even among other Nigerians, they claim that the 'always-Nigerian rule' does not apply to them. Without missing a beat, Kita promptly changes the rule to "whenever you are around me or your dad, you are in Nigeria."

The children are still trying to find ways of subverting this domestic dictatorship when Teni, her young daughter, comes across Bhully. To Teni, Bhully validates everything her mother has tried to inculcate in them, and she cannot wait to introduce Bhully to her mom.

"Mom, I met this woman today, and she is very African. I mean, she is from Nigeria," She quickly corrects herself before her mother mounts her soap box about how Africa is a continent of 52 countries, and about four times the size of the US. She does not want to dampen her enthusiasm.

"You will love her–She insists we call her "Aunty" and she makes us kneel to greet her," Teni hurries on breathlessly, blocking any space where her mom can interject.

Kita swallows hard and wonders what she has created; even her children don't kneel to her or their dad. That is one tradition about which she is ambivalent. Teni takes her mother's silence as encouragement, and she resumes her monologue, more slowly this time.

"She was very impressed that I knew how to kneel, and I did not question why I had to call her Aunty' when she is not related to me, and she wants to meet you. This is her number," Teni concludes in a rush, giving a piece of paper to her mother.

Kita takes the proffered paper, glances at it briefly, "Lady Bhully," she reads out with a chuckle, and promptly forgets all about her. Teni is confused and disappointed when three weeks later her mom still has not invited Bhully to their home.

About six months later, Kita spies a woman making a beeline for her as she leaves the post office.

"Excuse me please, ma'am," a woman's voice hails her in some slightly-off British accent, but it is neither forced nor false. Instinctively, Kita knows the owner of the voice is Bhully, and she makes a quick dash for her car, but not quick enough; Bhully has planted herself between Kita and the open door, before she can close it.

Impeccably dressed, Bhully is wearing about three African countries on her, each carefully calculated to accentuate her figure and bring out her smooth, dark skin. Her full luscious lips form an "O" scrunched with little side slits, her egg-like eyes expertly sweep right through her car before settling on Kita, finally.

"I am a hairdresser, dressmaker and maker of decorative arts. All my work use genuine African products," she says still with the slight British accent. "I moved into Littleville not too long ago, and I am trying to really make it real big in Lil. I realize you must be in a hurry and I don't want to keep you unnecessarily. Here is my card." She finishes by thrusting the card into Kita's face. Kita takes a brief look at it, just to confirm it is indeed, Lady Bhully, but before she can throw it in her cup-holder, her unwanted visitor continues.

"Actually, I too have finished at the post-office and if you don't mind, I will just hop into your car while we talk, and you can drop me off along the way."

Before Kita can recover from this presumptuous and brazen imposition on her time, Bhully is by the passenger door, rapping for Kita to open the door for her. Her head tilted at the angle of 'dare you mess with me,' is offset by those appealing egg-eyes that are all respectful. Kita, a student of human behavior and body language, is hooked. Who is this character! She does not have to wonder long. In what seemed like random conversation and small talks, first during the car ride, and later in many other, and increasingly frequent encounters, Kita learns more about her – at least what she decides to tell her, although she wonders how much of it is factual, and how much is the hustler's practiced survival yarn.

Bhully is one of the products of parental misguided good intentions gone horribly wrong. She comes from a very privileged and influential family in Nigeria; no event is complete in the circle of 'who is who' without her parents' presence. Interestingly, her parents were not born into wealth, and grew up dirt poor. It was with much struggle and determination that they finished high school where they met and fell in love. They got married soon after high school, the mother opting to be a stay-at-home wife, while the father worked diligently to become the CEO of the bank where he began as a lowly bank clerk. In no time, he opened his own bank, highly reputable, and one of the most solid in the country. Although her parents were strict, they were determined to protect their children from the deprivations they went through, and so spent lavishly on them. Nothing but the best for their three children, and every school vacation was spent somewhere in Europe. The children could not reconcile the social discipline with financial lavishness, and soon became a handful in their schools and upper-class neighborhood. The parents' misguided solution was to send them off to different 'boarding schools' in Europe to get "straightened up."

Bhully, the eldest of three, and her father's favorite, opts for America, where there are no established boarding schools as in Europe. At the tender age of fifteen, she flies to America where arrangements have been made to stay with a distant relative, who runs a sort of boarding house for African children studying in America. Sadly, it is the last place to provide structured guidance and focus for a young child; there is no supervision, and the children are left to their own devices. Bhully's stories of misadventures and misfortunes at this boarding place are endless and harrowing; it is a struggle for her to complete High School and gain admission to a Community College. After three dismal semesters, she drops out of school completely, and ultimately loses her student eligibility. To spare her parents the shame, she does not return home to Nigeria. The twists and turns of her experience and efforts to survive since constitute the perfect material for Kita's research on The Mental Impact of Children Studying Alone Abroad.

"What a boon!" she muses. She does not have to travel home to do her research; her research has come to find her. Before long, Kita is sponsoring many of Bhully's projects - day care service, hair saloon, restaurant business, etc. Each is a phenomenal failure, ruining in the process Kita's carefully managed credit history.

In no time, another expensive project presents herself to Kita. Out of nowhere the telephone rings.

"Hello?" answers Kita; she does not recognize the number. "Aunty, a long time no see.... How are you? This is Dollah. You remember? From years gone by at...."

Hun, hun..." Kita responds slowly and cautiously while she tries to switch on the computer in her head to run the memory database for voice, tone, inflection coming across the phone. It is all a buzz, no connection.

"I give you three guesses."

Kita hates the guessing game and is about to switch off the computer and end the call when the voice at the other end exclaims.

"Ha, Aunty! How can you forget Dollah with an 'h,' not dollar with an 'r,' at the end! Although I do not know who can do without the almighty dollar. Ha! ha!"

The computer in Kita's head quickly reboots itself, and right away, and all the data connect.

"Alert" flashes across the screen, in red, blinking furiously.

"Oh! my goodness! Dollah! I cannot believe this is you, after how many years?"

"At least twenty years," adds Dollah.

"I bet. Where on earth are you or coming from? What brings you to the US of A? What have you been doing with yourself? How did you get my number?"

"Ah, Aunty, my story, I can write a book."

The next twenty minutes, they are still on the phone, Dollah with an 'h' not dollar with an 'r' at the end dominating the conversation. Kita's attempt to grill Dollah and get a coherent story from her yields no result, Dollah expertly deflects her probing questions with, "Tory plenty, wey ah go tell all when ah see you." And she quickly goes back to her non-stop chatter, alternating between the good old times they had in their native land, when she served as Kita's field assistant, and all the indignities and suffering she has endured since migrating to America. As Dollah gets deeper in recounting her tales of woe, her voice becomes fainter, weepy, and she actually breaks down once. Kita eventually agrees to part with $300.00, so that Dollah can come for a short break, although she wonders, if she will be able to travel with all her medical problems. Instantly, Dollah's sniffling voice is transformed. It is now crisp, and business-like.

"You fit wire me the money today by Western Union? Se bi you know where him dey?"

"No. Where is it?"

"Haba, Aunty, you mean say you never wire money to anybody before?"

"No, I do bank transfers."

"Na wa o. Okay, at least you know Walmart."

As it happens, Kita was shopping at Walmart when the call came, so she carefully follows her instructions. To her amazement, the money is to be sent to Greyhound rather than to Dollah directly. Her curiosity to see Dollah increases, but when Dollah ends the phone still laughing over the fact that Kita has never used the Western Union, the computer in Kita's head starts beeping red Alert warning again.

Driving home, she wonders about Dollah, and her series of illnesses, and how she has been coping. The Dollah she remembers was a tough girl, but each time she tries to visualize her, it is Bhully's image that flashes across her vision. It is a ridiculous juxtaposition; they have nothing in common, she muses.

"I am sure they have never met each other, not here in the US, and definitely, not back home."

Unlike Bhully, Dollah grew up poor in one of the notorious slums of Lagos without the luxury of pampering from doting parents. An orphan, she learnt at an early age to fight tooth and nail for anything she wanted, a skill necessary for an even tougher future for dwellers of the slums. Whatever she has achieved has all been by dint of her own efforts; fortunately, she is enormously talented and creative. She is a self-made artist, but it has not been easy. Although her work has given her some international exposure, including meeting with some

African leaders, there is not enough market for her brand of performance, and so she lacks the financial resources to sustain the kind of life-style she desires. She frequently has to work odd jobs to meet basic needs, including as Kita's field assistant years back in Nigeria. Yes, she is also a hustler, like Bhully.

"Snap!" Kita jolts awake from her reverie. "That is the connection with the superimposed image of Bhully," Kita exclaims nodding her head vigorously as she pulls up her driveway and regrets that Dollah's illness will prevent the two hustlers from interacting.

Dollah breezes into town five days later with four suitcases, three duffel bags, and a tote bag. Thirty minutes later, Kita is at the Greyhound station ready to take Dollah home, but a huge surprise awaits her. Instead of a frail invalid, she is confronted with a bubbly Dollah in her element. She is in full performance before the motley crowd of passengers at the station, and they are eating out of her hand. She keeps them spell bound, but apparently, she is also on the lookout for Kita. For, as soon as Kita appears at the glass door of the station, rounds of clapping erupt from Dollah's small but appreciative audience, and she rushes to fling the door open.

"Aunty, welcome to Lil'! How I have missed you! Oh, Aunty you are looking so good! You have not changed at all."

She goes on as she drags Kita to the center of the room.

"Here is my Aunty I was telling you about. Without her, I will not exist. She is my everything. Please, help me thank her."

Another round of applause erupts from the paltry audience. As they start loading Dollah's suitcases and duffel bags into the trunk of the car, one of the Greyhound audience sidles up to Kita.

"I want to thank you personally for bringing Dollah to Lil.' She is going to liven up our town. Such a gem, such a gift, it is incredible. I hope she stays here for a long time. As soon as I get home, I am going to call all my groups in town and in church. We will line up speaking and performing engagements for her for the next twelve months. We want to keep her as long as we can.

Kita grinds her teeth, and says in her language, "Good luck – line up accommodation for her, and get her out of my skin."

"What did you say?" The woman wants to know.

"Fantastic! How wonderful!" Kita replied, trying hard to smile.

In the car, Kita cannot get over the contrast between the Dollah she has been expecting and the one now sitting smugly in her car. Dollah knows she has destabilized 'Aunty' with the scene at the station and has the upper hand of the situation. Kita needs desperately to come up with a plan, a workable strategy, urgently, before she gets home, and for this she needs some space and time to think. She decides to take the longest route home to buy time, but first, deflate the one now sitting smugly next to her and stop her chatter.

"I thought you said you have been sick and close to death several times."

"You know me, Aunty. I cannot be down for long. I have to keep moving, it is just my nature. I have surprised the doctors many times, too."

"That's right, and that was quite a performance at the station."

"Aunty, I cannot help it, performance is in my blood, in fact..."

"Indeed, you have not changed." Kita cuts her off harshly. "Now tell me, exactly why you are here," Kita continues. "It is obvious you have not just come on a casual visit. How long were you waiting at the station that you already lined up engagements for a year? Obviously, you are prepared for a long stay judging by you being here with seven suitcases."

"No. Four, Aunty! The rest are tote bags."

Kita continues as if she had not spoken. "Are you sure you did not have contacts here before you contacted me? And my role is to provide you with accommodation and transportation? In fact, how am I sure the crowd at the Station were not your groupies who travelled with you from New York, and what I witnessed there was not all orchestrated for me?"

"As to God who made me, Aunty, you know I will never deceive you or anything like that."

Kita wants to remind Dollah of the gold and silver jewelry sets she promised to sell for Kita's friend, but both the jewelry and money disappeared into thin air. Kita quietly paid her friend, who had brought them from Dubai to help finance her trip to, and resume her studies in, the U.S.A. But she decides against it. Mistake. Dollah takes the hesitation to launch her tales of woe, but Kita, tired of being taken for a sucker, impatiently shuts her up.

"Save it, now be quiet, and tell me everything you have been up to since you have been in this country."

Dollah joined a famous musician and his band on a cultural trip tour to America with the tacit understanding he would make her his third wife, once the tour was over. To her shock, he married the white woman who had been helping him to put the tour together, and who functioned as his Public Relations Officer (PRO) in the U.S.A. Dollah did not mind being wife number four, but the white woman did not understand the concept of co-wife and would have none of it. The poor woman actually believed she was the only wife, and her husband, a widower. Although she had been to Nigeria a couple of times, she thought the other two wives were her husband's big sister and young niece. That was ten years ago, and Dollah had moved on, but remained in the U.S.A.

"These men!" Kita hissed. Then she continues in a soft sympathetic voice.

"So, what have you been doing since, apart from your hospital rounds? Or have you been sick every day for ten years?"

Silence. Kita continues.

"You know, Dollah, no matter who you are, once you migrate, it is back to school, all over again, and get your B.A. in any field."

"Aunty! Go back to school? I am over 45!" Dollah replied.

"And so? How many times have I told you, you are never too old to learn? Have you forgotten? Don't tell me that since you have been in this country you have never come across stories of men and women in their 60s, 70s and 80s going back to school to earn the degree or that High School Diploma they have always wanted? Some parents are even in the same class as their children."

"Yes, but where ah go get the money? You know our situation as immigrants is different; we are dealing with too many issues."

"Precisely! Your immigrant status is your 'get-back-to-school' decree for a mandatory B.A. – Begin Again degree."

"Oh, Aunty, you still dey get time to joke! Ah think say you dey talk about real university degree, ah for fear, when ah no even finish secondary school!" A brief pause, then:

"Ah don dey here ten years now, at least, when ah go get my B.A.? Abi, how many years him dey take?"

"Until you stop being an immigrant and you go back home."

Kita stops talking, and waits for Dollah's response, but only silence answers her back. Suddenly, it dawns on Kita that Dollah is probably an undocumented immigrant, just like Bhully. She has to revise her strategy. Kita takes a side road that leads her back to Lil' town, and deliberately drives through the more depressed area of Lil.' The rest of the trip home is in silence, broken only by heavy sighs from Dollah. But, Kita ignores the bait and refuses to enquire from her passenger the cause of the sighs. Instead, as they drive past the city hospital, Kita resumes talking.

"Seriously, you should have retrained, learnt something – that is how to survive. Nursing, for example, and you have the brains; there is a serious shortage of nurses everywhere, and they command top money.

"God forbid! Ah be artist to the core."

"Now, I think I know what your problem is. Laziness."

Kita drives up to her garage door and switches off the engine.

"Wey your second car, Aunty?"

"This here is my only car."

"This one wey we dey inside? Na wa o!"

Kita decides to ignore her, but feels more confident her new plan will work.

"Leave the suitcases for now; we will get them later after dinner."

Barely five minutes after dinner the doorbell rings. Dollah dashes to the door. Kita deliberately gives her about a minute before following her. She is certain it is Bhully at the door, and she wants them to get acquainted with each other on their own terms, without a third party intruding. She stands slightly behind watching them as they study and size each other up, silently. Then, seconds later, Bhully and Dollah burst into an explosive laughter, simultaneously. Kita lets out a huge sigh of relief. Apparently, she had been holding her breath.

"I see you kindred spirits have done your introductions. Perfect! You can fill in the details on your way home, and in coming days or months. Dollah's suitcases are still in my car, you can start unloading into Bhully's van now."

"Aunty, she is staying with me?" Asks Bhully, incredulously.

"Aunty, I am staying with her?" Dollah enquires, not believing her ears.

"You are both right," Kita answers, leading them resolutely towards the garage. "When story meets performer, it is a show! And this pod here is not big enough."

Ada Uzoamaka Azodo

Ada Uzoamaka Azodo, Ph.D., educator, literary and cultural critic, writer, feminist theorist, teaches and researches in African, African American and African Diaspora Studies, and Women's and Gender Studies in the Humanities. Dr. Azodo is affiliated with Indiana University Northwest and Purdue University Northwest. Her books and book chapters on classical Francophone and Anglophone African authors abound in critical anthologies with Peter Lang, Africa World Press, Lexington Books, Oxford University Press, and other publishers. Peer-reviewed articles are also available in hard copies and online in notable academic journals. Dr. Azodo's magnum opus, *L'imaginaire dans les romans de Camara Laye*, is a unique study on spirituality, legends and myths in African and African American cultures. Volume Advisor for "Aminata Sow Fall: Senegalese Novelist and Short Story Writer," in *Contemporary Literary Criticism*, Gale Cengage Learning, Azodo also founded the "Immigrant Voices in Short Stories" creative writing group that allows its members to present their compositions at the African Literature Association annual conferences. An advocate of gender equality in opportunities, Dr. Azodo has propounded a feminist theory, "Di-feminism" that valorizes the indigenous Igbo concept of Agunwanyị (Lion-Woman), in *African Feminisms in the Global Arena: Novel Perspectives on Gender, Class, Ethnicity, and Race*. A life member of the African Literature Association (ALA), the Modern Languages Association (MLA), African Studies Association (ASA), and the Flora Nwapa Society, Dr. Azodo is also a member of Conseil International d'Études Francophones (CIÉF), American Association of Teachers of French (AATF), Literary Society of Nigeria (LSN), Association of African Women Scholars (AAWS), and currently two-term President of the Igbo Studies Association (ISA) of North America. Dr. Azodo's scholarship has been recognized in the Cambridge International Biography by "Cambridge Who's Who," in "Who's Who in American Education," "Who's Who in the World of Women," and since 1994 as a V.I.P. listee in the "Marquis Who's Who." In 2019, Dr. Azodo received the Albert Nelson Marquis Lifetime Achievement Award for her longevity in scholarship. Another Lifetime Achievement Award cum Honorary Chieftaincy title, "Ada-Di-Ebube" (Distinguished Daughter), has come from her natal town of Amawbia, Anambra State, Nigeria. Dr. Azodo was a nominee for the Indiana University Northwest 2019 Founders' Day Excellence in Teaching Award.

Seven

Her Purple Huffy

IT WAS THE FIRST SUMMER AFTER OUR return in the winter following a five-year sojourn in Nigeria. Finally, we were able to scrape together enough money to get a bicycle for our daughter. She had longed for it all her six years of existence on earth at the time. Now, I'm exaggerating a little here, of course, for she knew nothing of bicycles as a baby! But, seriously, we had heard daily of this particular need of hers for so long that we were literally running crazy hearing about it. Her plea for a bike intensified once we got back to the country and she could see that getting her dream toy was a doable proposition. That morning, on his way out to work, Dad counted out all the money needed for the purchase and handed it to me. The routines over with the children, I set out with our daughter to Toys-"R"-Us for the very important buy. I was determined to return from the toy store in good time to collect her siblings that went to grade school from the bus.

Since the day I found out, to my shock, the reason Tai trailed home long after his siblings were back, I had added to my routines the one of picking up the children from the school bus. I was more shocked than annoyed that not he, Tai, nor Kehin, his twin brother, nor their other two older siblings, revealed to me the true story of his predicament. I also wondered about why Tai, the darker-skinned one, was picked on, but not Kehin with the lighter skin color. After all, they were of the same age, size and in the same grade. Did this really have something to do with his skin color? Why did the bully pick on Tai? Five times, already, it was the same scenario; he trailed back home long after his siblings. The sixth time was when I went to the bus stop to find out for myself why he came back late to the house after he got off the bus. And, lo and behold, hiding behind the bushes, he was dodging a predator to which he had fallen prey. A real beast he was in human disguise, this bully that stalked my son. He had a large head, bow legs and piercing balls of fire for eyes in his ocular orbits. I shouted at the menace, and dared him to lay his ugly claws again on my son. Surprised, he took off and sprinted away to the safety of his home. I followed suit. At his aged grandparents' house, I swore that if I saw again what I had seen happen I was going to huff and I was going to puff and I was going to blow someone's house down and I would maim somebody.... At my swearing, the grandparents quaked with a mighty consternation. Believe it or not, the grandparents felt quite threatened and missed nothing of my state of annoyance and frustration. Next, it was my turn to take pity on the poor grandparents after listening to some of the discipline problems with their ward. I, a parent myself, I apologized to them for losing my cool. After all, I should have been more civilized than those I was chastising for their bad behavior!

That was the first time I ever saw and met the grandparents and their bully of a grandson. I discovered into the bargain the reason they took on his parenting; to contribute to turning him around into the straight and narrow path of discipline and usefulness to himself and the community. You see, they retrieved him from his single mother, their daughter, who worked three full-time jobs in an inner city, to nurture and give him an opportunity for better education from a better neighborhood school than his single parent could afford in her dwelling and the school system to which they were tied. But, the leopard cannot change its spots, they say. Having been used to street fighting for survival, he would not stop. He would get off the bus and as soon pursue my son with the darker skin as he descended the bus and tried to get home. The hide and seek would continue, my son trying to dodge the bully that was in hot pursuit by hiding behind bushes, until he found the safe space to sprint home.

So, the drama over that day, we walked home, my son and I. I was glad that we had put paid to the bully problem. That late afternoon, though, as I got ready to prepare dinner, I learned from him and his other siblings that they did not want to raise issues about Tai's pseudo truancy lest they provoked a fight between the parents. They also hoped that the bullying would go away, when they became better acquainted with one another. But, what did they know, children that they were, about the imperative to fight back when neighbors trespass behind your backyard in order to close it, as our elders would say?

Back to the store meanwhile at Toys-"R"-Us that shopping day, a store hand diligently helped us, my daughter and I, to pick out the right size of bicycle for her. All was going well at that point and the store hand expected us to proceed to payment, until I asked him to kindly open the large box and put the bike parts together for us. I was not given at all to mechanical ability.

"Woman, do you have a husband?" was his angry retort.

I did not respond, tired I was of consistently being asked many times in the stores this sort of question. My facial gestures must have betrayed my exhaustion and shame, though I perfectly understood his point of view. For many an American man, husband and dad, handy to a fault, putting together the parts from a box—toys, furniture, etc.—was a non-issue…. His demeanor also somewhat showed he understood well my predicament. The woman, with an accent, what does she know? Almost immediately in spite of himself he became somewhat regretful of his uncouth question. Now, that's also his American side. For an extra fee of $10.00, he proceeded to put the bike together for us for the next one hour or so. The task accomplished and without further ado, he handed us her purple huffy. He again apologized for his bad attitude towards me at the beginning. And we wheeled the beauty, the lovely, the royal machine away, out of the store, and to the car, and sped home.

We were hardly parked than my daughter descended on me to bring down her huffy, so that she could try it.

"Mom, hurry up! I want to see if I can ride it!"

As I watched her pedal hesitantly, but happily, down the sidewalk of the apartment complex towards Elmwood Avenue, my mind digressed into past times. Reflections on fate and destiny succeed one another as they populate my mind. First, the drudgery of the days with invariable routines hovering over children at breakfast, lunch and dinner; helping them with homework; escorting them to the playground, and walking them back home from the school bus. What a life! A life uniquely in service to others, so to say, through and through! Oh, and the waiting for Dad to come home for dinner at the end of the work day! Yup, we all called him Dad, including myself for, for our family unit he was the Alpha and the Omega, and the beginning and the end. His return signaled a chance for family life to finally begin as the sun went down, family life that would end almost as abruptly as it began because everyone would need to go to bed and get some sleep before the next day came around, again, the next day of the same drudgery and the same routines.

Then, second, the days at university studying to earn the baccalaureate degree made their way into view. To help move the world forward, yes, perhaps, to make a difference! Why not? A foreign language degree was superbly *rentable*, as the French would say. You could do whatever you wanted to do with the magic of the ability to speak it and present the culture of people who spoke it to others. Even as a spontaneous interpreter! Nigeria was surrounded by French neighbors and one could disappear there and not feel lost like less common folks would be. The world was a mystery to be explored and you fitted right in.

Then, oh! The amorous escapades and the sexcapades invade your psyche next! Yep! Those were good times, too. It was surely good to be young. What was good for the goose was also good for the gander. Didn't Karmen Geï say so, that many women often feel like men, but just do not acknowledge their feelings? Or rather that society forbids them to do that? So, they go around, morose, and denying their God-given intense sexual nature? At least, our people who instituted excision knew that a woman could be as sexually wild as a man. Any wonder they thought of clitoral amputation? To tame the shrew? So, if modern women think that they are sexually endowed as men, the ancients thought differently; they did not allow two mad people to coexist in the same house or their home would go up in flames! That was their reasoning. The female was made to settle down to wifehood and motherhood, and tending to the home, through the practice of excision, leaving the male to continue to sow his wild oaks, even after marriage, until perhaps impotence set in. He could acquire as many wives as he wanted, without being satisfied with his harem. It did not matter to his community. He could continue to menace young girls the age of his own adult children, with cultural acceptance and praise for his virility. That was *the* rationale for instituting the practice of clitoridectomy; to have at least one sane mind in the household. Strange cultural ideas, wouldn't you say!? Or, were they?

Hmm, time was up for all frivolities, you had to forgo so-called childish things.... Now, look at an adult in the mouth and you find it hard to believe he or she also sucked at the mother's breast! Oh, to explore your feelings and your body, again, to explore into the bargain the bodies of other people in your sphere of influence! Those are now bygones in the realm of dreams! For, all that had to end after a certain time! Alas! Things had to change as you got serious about the future. For, being really, finally adult meant thinking of the future.

Next, search for a career after studies to settle into trouble your mind. You could go and get a law degree and function as a company secretary, earn big, and drive big foreign cars, read American cars. If you preferred, you could train as a manager of a bank, and there were quite a few of them in Lagos those days that wanted new graduates with foreign language expertise as trainee managers. And you would have had it made with ability to earn well and have extra means to support the needy of your friends and extended family. Teaching was also an option, be it in the secondary school or at the university level, though it would not pay so well. But then, there is the possibility of becoming a Professor! The almighty professor, a very much respected profession like that of a judge in Nigeria! Even doctors would ditch their medical training and expertise for a chance to be called a Professor! At university, you'd first start as a lecturer, then go for your M.A. (Master's), M.Phil. (Master of Philosophy) or proceed to work for your Ph.D. (Doctor of Philosophy), if your thesis proved too large for a mere Master of Philosophy. But marriage, marriage was a third option. You exercised that third option.

Yep! The somewhat little life of marriage comes up into mind. Really a small life, it was. But, you knew your people expected it. Your parents conditioned you for it right from the beginning of your arrival into existence and would be thoroughly disappointed, would feel greatly disgraced, if it did not happen. And inwardly you wanted to go that way to feel fulfilled. There was the possibility, you considered, of having children to whom to bequeath your legacy at the end of the day. There was also the hope for support, under oath of allegiance, of course, from your partner as an added value and benefit, in sickness and in health, in poverty and in wealth, in plenty and penury, till the end of your days on earth. It was a hope, for you have seen friends who got married, but with whom you would not have wanted to trade places. Marriage would mean a smaller life, surely, compared to other options, but it was a life that promised shelter from loneliness and isolation, especially when you were aged or down and out. Yes, it was a different kind of life that no other option could afford you. Ever since a young age, it had been drummed into your psyche that that was what all respectable men and women worth their salt in your culture did. You would be a failure to yourself and society, if you did not get married. As your people would tell a good girl, it was imperative for her to look for a worthy husband for herself and a capable father to take care of her children. "Start early to look for the black goat, for at night it might be impossible for you to find it," they would tell her as a proverbial piece of advice. The potential of a fat bank account to your name would not be a substitute. All notwithstanding, *you* did not want to fail.

Continuing, your mind rakes up the past and you mull the dichotomy of love and respect in your culture and other foreign traditions. In African and Jewish traditions, for example, they hold that it is a man's love for his wife that matters, for it alone sustains a marriage. The woman only owes respect to her man. If a man loses his love for his wife, they hold, the marriage crumbles, for his wife's respect cannot sustain their relationship. There will be other women that would be only too glad to step in and do the man's biddings. In Jewish tradition often quoted and related in the Bible, husbands are enjoined to love their wives and the wives are to respect their husbands. No more, no less. Then, in Igbo tradition, the ancients advocated the concept and practice of suitor, as opposed to date and dating. That is to say that a man made himself first, meaning, cultivated skills in farming, hunting, fishing or other occupation, built his man's hut, and then was ready to pick a wife. On the other hand, the young woman was raised by her mother to prepare for marriage, by learning to cook, clean, and care for children, and then to wait for a suitable suitor to come. She had to wait, the young woman, and picked her partner from the array of suitors that came to her father's compound to knock on the door and ask for her hand in marriage. But, all that changed. With Western-style education, young women began to propose love and marriage to young men, on their own initiative and terms, and at their peril sometimes.

Woes betide you, if your husband has many sisters, especially when father luck has not helped them to find husbands of their own. How friends envied you when it came to pass that your family was going to travel to the diaspora. One exclaimed, wishing she were in your shoes, "You have escaped, and, oh, you have escaped them! Do not forget me! Pray for me!" Yep! She was right, for it was a clean escape for you. You had shared your woes, when sisters-in-law dumped themselves on you during their frequent visits, unannounced, of course, and their bewildered brothers were incapable of shooing them off. They did not come singly, no o. They came in groups of two or three, literally in droves, to lend force of number to their machinations, and so cower you into temerity. The distance across the miles did not always shield you from their onslaught either. Even from that far distance, they hauled insults in stinkers they sent, wondering which devil in their brother's house was stopping him from sending them more sustenance money than was sent to them from your meager resources from time to time. Afterall, you were in America, the land of milk and honey! Marriage had become an ordeal of sorts. So, being in good accord with the one you love, against all odds, was of primary importance, if not of the only importance.

Eh, unbelievable! Standing there in the middle of the sidewalk, I was still lost in thoughts reminiscing the past, when the sight of my daughter shouting and pedaling furiously back up the turn from the portion of Elmwood Avenue that led to our apartment complex brought me back to the present. I shook my head to shake off my state of stupor. Unbelievable! How many thousands of miles back into the past I traveled in mid-afternoon and within a very short spate of time standing in a sidewalk! I shook my head again to clear it of the fog that threatened to overwhelm it. It was all a daydream, then? Thank God! Glad to be back to the present again, I realized my daughter was beckoning to me.

"Mom! Mom! Mom! I just talked to a cop. I talked to a cop," she was saying.

"Okay. You spoke to a policeman," I rejoined, struggling to be present and not quite sure how to respond to her excitement.

"Yeah! He was going down Elmwood in his police car. He was on the other side of the street. He was looking at me. I…, I… did not know what to do. I…, I… quickly got off my bike. And I…, I…, I stood at attention beside my bike. And I was watching the cop. Then, the cop turned around in his car. Then, the cop…, the cop came towards me. The cop came, s-l-o-w-l-y," she added, quite pent up.

I took a deep breath, and I tried to calm her down.

"All right, and the Officer came towards you slowly. What did he do after he came towards you? Did he talk to you? What did he say to you…?"

"He slowed down. He smiled. He waved to me."

"Okay! Okay! He slowed down, he smiled and he waved to you …. And then, what else did he do, the Officer?"

"And then he drove off towards Twelve Corners."

Then, holding the area of her heart as one would do with utter relief after an excruciating experience, she blurted out, "Oh, I thought he was going to give me a ticket!"

"A ticket!?" I asked, utterly amazed, flabbergasted. "You thought he was going to give you a ticket? What for? What did you do? Do you even know the speed limit on Elmwood?"

"Yeah, 35 mph," she responded, deadpan.

I was speechless. *Conversation à bâtons rompus*! I was dumbfounded! I collected my daughter and we went back home, she biking her purple huffy and I walking beside her. In mute wisdom, it dawned on me at that moment that life could be really exhilarating, if we lived it in the moment, just like a child.

Eight

A Wake in Chytown

MATAROR AND OGENE LISTSERVS HAD SPREAD THE news far and wide that a dearly beloved mother, mother-in-law, and grandmother back home was about to be sent in grand style to the land of the dead.

The Wake for the Celebration of Life scheduled to begin at seven o'clock p.m. that Saturday evening fills up three-quarters closer to ten o'clock p.m. The venue at 26th and Michigan, as it is popularly known, which is normally designated for no more than two hundred fifty persons is breaking at the seams with some three times its capacity, not counting the children of all ages whose domain is the adjoining streets and the parking lot in front of the hall. The local police would come in intermittently to beseech parents to secure their children or they would be arrested. And I have never seen the police so indulgent, for their threat is proffered but not executed. So, the parents hear the injunction with one ear and allow it to float out through the other ear.

It is a hot and humid summer evening. Inside, wake attendees are sweating profusely like sheep as the air-conditioners hum fruitlessly to cool the hall. The two opposite ends of the dance floor situated in the middle of the room are packed with mourners. Others not able to find chairs to sit on are sitting on the window ledges, and still others are on the floor with their backs to the wall for support. The bereaved, their close relatives and friends, are decked out in gorgeous aṣọ-ébi made hurriedly but superbly for the occasion. They look splendid in the color coordination of purple and black wrapper and orange blouse with matching purple gélé. Other groups of friends have also chosen for themselves a uniform of orange headscarves or any other colors agreed upon.

This uniform palaver, though, is always the problem of the women, for the men do not care. They just do not put themselves in any kind of uniform most of the time. Only occasionally, a group of men would wear similar pocket scarves to identify as belonging to the same club as the chief male mourner. They prance around on the dance floor, showing off male strength, vigor and solidarity.

In the brouhaha that summer evening, everyone is really waiting for the end of the short, 30-minute Service of Songs in honor of the dead, before the miliki begins, which is the real thing for the evening. It is a party, a big one. Whoever thinks it is a solemn occasion because someone died is in for a rude deception. Finally, the long-awaited announcement from the MC comes through the mic.

"Ụmụnne m na Ụmụnna m, ndewo nụ o!

Ladies and gentlemen, good evening!

I salute you all again!

Please get up and go get yourself some food to eat. We have plenty and you can go as many times as you like. There is plenty of moin-moin, jollof rice, fried rice with shrimp, mixed meat (goat, chicken, turkey, and others), fried fish, vegetable soup, vegetable salad, legumes, fresh fruits trays, chin-chin, puff-puff, and meatpies. There are also assorted drinks: bottled water, Heineken, Budweiser light beer, red wine and white wine, Guinness stout, Hennessey, Irish cream, coke, sprite, Schweppes lemon, Pepsi, malt. You name it, and we have it...!

Ladies and gentlemen, we are gonna have a good time tonight!"

People stopped listening to the tedious litany a long time ago. But, the MC was doing his job. A glance at the clock announces twelve midnight or a time very close to it. Many are hungry, even if they had some form of dinner before their arrival. The combination of heat and commotion makes you want to go eat again. What else is there really to do? Food and good company are the real reasons majority of the people are there. Priests and nuns are not left behind either, for after saying the opening prayers and a short homily for the repose of the dead, they too fall to. A long line immediately forms as attendees await their turn to get their food and and dig into it.

Then, among the slow coaches like me, who would rather wait for the throng to thin down a bit before going for their food, I think I overhear an interesting conversation at some point. I feel constrained to eavesdrop in spite of myself. I strain my ears and I do indeed overhear a dirty gossip going on between some ladies close to me.

"This wake is really going to be something else," says a lady in a low tone to a group of her friends. "I hear that only the husband is going home for the funeral, even though the obituary flyer says the whole family is going. Chei! Our people! Tụfia kwa!"

"Yes, o. Na so I see am o. Dem surprise you, our people? You talk as if to say you no know our people again," interjects a second lady.

"Ah! Na so I hear am o, me one ...," continues the first lady who spoke. "Se be na so. Ah, our people? Forget them. Only de person way no know dem go wonder. Dem jus' wan make plenty money for dis town all the time. Finish!"

"Bo, wetin man go do? Wetin you dey talk, my sistas? Tief, abanị-dị-egwu, dat na we. Na so so poach poach for anoda man pocket," cuts in a third lady. "Trow big party for family member wey pass for home. Den, do de job, je-je."

"Wo, my sister. E be like dem go go treat demself to better 'oliday after," cuts in again the second lady.

"'Oliday, ke! 'Oliday, ko! 'Oliday, ni! 'Oliday wey dem no fit pay for before since dem dey work since fifteen years for dis contri...." It is the first lady again speaking.

"Ah, you luck out, if dem save de loot small for sen' home to de people wey need de money for plan the burial ceremony," rejoins the second lady.

"Hmm, Me one ...," the first lady begins to say, "I hear say dat Okiwe Aduba don begin small business cleaning office with him booty from last year wake for him sista...."

"Hein! Chei! Chei! Wonda shall nefer end," interjects the third lady.

"At least him invest de money wisely, abi? No be say like him squander am," the second lady explains. "At least dat don end him joblessness. Him go earn money for take care of himself and his shildren. E be like community fund. Wit de money wey him rob people finish, him go fit employ himself and help oder people ...," she concludes.

"Don't forget the issue of Committee of Friends," pontificates a fourth lady. "Hear ye all, my people! We don't levy people; we don't commercialize death where we come from! We know our moral obligations to the needy in times of distress! All, according to the weight of our individual pockets! Everyone pitches in, according to his or her means to help out the grieving! Therein lies, and only therein lays the joy and fulfillment of gift giving! Amen! Ekenekwaa m unu o." So be it!

Hmm, Hmm, I think. The audacity!

At that point another distraction calls away my attention. The dinner is going nicely; several people that have eaten or are waiting to get their food are spending their time gyrating on the dance floor in the middle of the hall to breathtaking music from the DJ's machine. And I watch them with great amusement, wondering what they would really look like without the sound of music from the DJ's machine. Like some odd creatures, throwing their distal, middle, and proximal phalanges here and there, left and right, ridiculously!

A wake in Chytown is indeed something to behold. As the event is happening, quite a few people are going around saluting their friends and acquaintances. Others are doing business, including distributing flyers for upcoming events, such as baby showers, bridal showers, other wakes, fundraising, and more. Chytown-style wakekeeping is an excellent opportunity to see fellows at their best and worst. At their best, they commiserate with one another; support one another in cash and kind, as fellow strangers in a foreign land. At their worst, they make believe to mourn with you and also mourn themselves and their helplessness in the diaspora. They mourn the old back home that need good healthcare that they cannot get. Alas!

Older and younger Nigerians are beginning to die off in Chytown, due to stress and mental health issues. Soon, very soon, old peoples' homes will be calling Nigerians in the diaspora. They are not quite ready to transition back to the old country to age and die, for back home is fast becoming a place unknown, where they would recognize only a few people, if any at all, where the young would not know who they are, and where they would lack the level of healthcare to which they have gotten used abroad. So, Chicagoans gloat with pseudo happiness, in order to dull their nerves with the celebration of the passing of yet another beloved relative back home. At the wake, they are all dressed up and fill their stomach with eating and drinking. They show off their new attires, and they dance the night away to cap it all. They slap the hands of family, friends and acquaintances with joy and gladness as they meet them while comingling.

The slurping of food and the downing of drinks almost over, the voice of the MC comes again over the mic....

"Are we all having a good time?"

"Yeeees!" echo the attendees.

"Are we all having a splendid time? he asks a second time.

"Yeee, yeeeees!" respond the crowd enthusiastically, half asleep or drunk or both.

"Are we all calling on God to be merciful on the soul of our dearly beloved sister? ..."

His questions are redundant. This third time, the audience screams the response. "Yeeeeeeeeeees! Yesssss! Yeeeees o!" The voices are coming from all corners of the room at the same time, and quite discordantly.

"What we are witnessing today, my brothers and sisters, is a celebration of life," continues the MC. "Ladies and gentlemen ..."

The Deejay drowns out his voice with bellows from his computer of the song "Sweet Mother, I no go forget you..."

The gathering throngs onto the dance floor once more and digs down.

Several weeks ago, *Matador* and *Ogene*, the two online organs that Chytown embraces, like the traditional town criers of old had faithfully relayed far and wide the news of the impending gathering. In the days leading up to the event, again and again, the message dished out the fear of Armageddon, should people fail to turn up for the wake.

"Chicago & Environs!

Our sister Ezinne are survived by seven children, including our very own Honorable Mr. Okeke Okonkwo and Chief Dr. Augustine Okonkwo (Sons), and Mrs. Justina Okonkwo (daughter-in-law). Born to Gilbert & Mary Ofianagbaozala of Umuochi-Umakwa, Anambra State, she grew to be bigger than his father and mother. She's survive her husband Mr. Nwokonkwo Nweke, 7 children, including our very own Honorable Okeke Okonkwo, the President of Aganaba Men's Social Club of Chicago town."

The grammar is entirely his.

Dance time, again. The gathering has come alive after a little exercise that helped the contents of their digestive system to settle. This time, they deliberately dance energetically to burn off more of the excess calories. This time, it is "M.O.N.E.Y." by Timaya and Flavour. Like the High-Life music of the good oldtimes, it is loud and beckoning the dancers onto the dance floor with its fire.

Every night and day the boy dey fly to Dubai
All the way from Naija to just go flenjor for Dubai

I travel to America just to go charge my phone

Bad belle people make una leave me alone
I say when money no dey
People dey carry me play

When money no dey

Everybody run away
I say when money no dey no no no

People dey use me dey play
When money no dey
Nobody look at my face
Orugo

Them feeling them feeling them feeling
Them feeling them feeling the boy
The ladies The ladies The ladies
The ladies them wanting the boy
When the going is too damn good
Many many people will be your friend

It is mainly the women, however, who dance. They dance provocatively among themselves, since the men would rather continue drinking alcohol than dance with their wives or other female friends or acquaintances. They touch their breasts and buttocks in utter mimickry of sexual activity, as if to taunt their men or make them jealous and so bring them out to the floor.

But, of course, the men disregard them and continue to drink as if there would be no tomorrow. That is the manly thing to so, they believe. The womanly thing is to dance. Can't believe their voluptuous stimulation at the sound of M.O.N.E.Y! It is money, abi? Always money! These women....

Every hour has seen the pouring in of a steady flow of more and more sympathizers or mourners. I see the organizers carting away some of the excess food in chaffing dishes and drinks in cartons to their waiting cars in the parking lot. The MC is now announcing the order in which groups will come to the high table to pay their respects to the bereaved family.

"Our people, olue nu n'omume o!

We all knows why we are here. We are here at this wake keeping and celebration of life for our sister to help our own sister and brother at their times of needs. Hon. Okeke Okonkwo and his wife are a pillar and they always helps to uplift people in our Nigerian community of Chicago & its Environs. This is also a fundraising. Please dip into your pocket and come up to the table and meet us here. We are here and we will help you offload. They helps everybody in this community. Now it is their turns. Please come forward. Tank you!"

Pay no attention to the grammar mistakes you perceive in the announcement or you might find yourself doubting the value of your secondary school education. Seriously!

Meanwhile, first on the floor is Mrs. Nwanyimgbo, the Ogidigbo of Ebenebe 1 of Anyafulukwe, in honor of her mother-in-law. She is determined to demonstrate her grief at the passing of her mother-in-law. She is holding an eight by ten framed photograph of the dearly beloved departed in front of her as she moves in rhythm to the befitting music of such an elder wafting from the Deejay's machine. Her lady friends and family dance around her while she dances in the middle of the circle. Sympathizers spray her with dollar notes in her honor and to contribute to the expenses of the evening. It is for moments like this that many Chicago women take out membership in several organizations, in many more than they can possibly be active members and still do the jobs that pay them salaries. Husbands spray their dancing wives and spray the dancing bereaved daughter-in-law. Periodically, Nwanyi lets out a soulful wail to show her sorrow at the passing of so great a mother-in-law, a good woman, good mother, Ezinne, Nne Oma, who knew her family, loved and nurtured its members beyond imagination. Soon, dollar notes litter the dance floor and are dutifully collected by designated friends and relatives in used grocery plastic bags. They first sweep dollar notes together with a broom with a long handle and then they get small children to pick them up and stuff them into plastic bags. The notes are then packed into bundles of ten and twenty, from which selected members of the family and trusted friends sitting prominently upfront on a pre-arranged table make change for others waiting to break their bigger bills, so that they too can spray the dancers. Then, other social groups to which the woman belongs also come to dance in their turn. Finally, the men's dance brings up the rear of the dance groups on the list, with its energetic moves and boisterousness in support of the grieving man of the day. That the man has paid his dues by supporting many in the community over three decades is evident. It is a big business, the party, the dancing the spraying and the sweeping up of the wake harvest of dollar notes. If the MC thinks that not enough notes have been collected for the evening to be worth it, he invariably continues calling out more subgroups to dance and pay their respects to the bereaved.

"My people please get up and hit the dance floor en mass to support and appreciate the unquestionable loyalty of this man who been there for us in good and bad times in the community. May the Raisin God take good care of you BUNCH."

The (mis)spellings are also reflections of the soundings of his speech.

Obediently, wake goers walk up intermittently to the table set aside in the corner to have their donations and pledges dutifully recorded in the book by one of the committee of friends. In future, those records would be consulted to decide whether to bother to support Mr, Mrs. or Ms So, So and So in their own times of need. Some of the pledges, however, will never be redeemed. After one or two attempts to collect, due to the unresponsiveness of the pledger, the 'creditors' will give up. Some would rationalize in sympathy, asking—"O ji nke ya" (Does he have his own?) In English-speak, it means, 'whoever collected from a Church mouse?' In that way, they register their discontent with many a life of wretchedness that some of our people live in Chytown. Alas! Only a small fraction of the booty will be delivered to the bereaved after all the food, drinks and music expenses are paid for and the sum subtracted to the minutest detail.

4:30 am. Sunday morning, already!

Wake goers now spent from overeating, over drinking and exertion are leaving for home to get much needed rest and sleep. Sometimes, it takes an hour to untangle the cars that have been parked haphazardly during the party. Some, who had wanted to leave earlier, about 2:00 a.m., were not able to do so, because the owners of the cars parked in front of theirs could not be found. Not all the announcements for owners of cars blocking people could bring out the drivers to move their cars. Alas! Then, finally able to leave, some have gotten into car accidents on their way back home after such late-night revels. Alas!

6:00 am.

The die-hards of the men remain to finish off as much of the alcohol left as they can. They outdo one another, drinking. The leftovers are collected and saved by the committee of friends. Finally, the bereaved family packs up their belongings and drags their half-dead bodies to the parking lot to go home. They will wake up towards the evening and do their accounting. Then, the clarity of the wake will come into focus; it has been a grand party for the diaspora community, but not nearly enough money picked up for their immediate needs for the roundtrip journey home and back to do real honor to their defunct relative.

To wit, there is no end to town unions upon town unions formed ostensibly to socialize and support one another in foreign land, but which turn out many times to be avenues for collecting money. It is not farfetched to say that—and this has happened quite a few times--a clique would make away with money contributions from all members and damn the consequences. They dare the group to take them to court. Alas! In the spirit of solidarity, no one does anything like that; either they are too busy trying to make money at their jobs or they are at a loss as to what to do. Going to court is the last option on their minds. Who would bell the cat? Who would really want to have it said on record that he or she, a bona fide African, dragged his own brother or sister to court in foreign land? So, the vivious cycle continues unabbated!

No wonder Chytowners do outrageous things to hold on to their wake loot for oiling their lives in hostland.

Pede Hollist

Arthur Onipede Hollist, aka Pede Hollist, PH.D., is a Professor of English at The University of Tampa (UT), Florida, U.S.A., and an award-winning fiction writer who teaches African literature and creative writing. His credits include *So the Path Does Not Die*, named the 2014 African Literature Association Creative Book of the Year; "Foreign Aid," shortlisted for the 2013 Caine Prize and published in *A Memory This Size and Other Stories;* and "The Tale of the Three Water Carriers," longlisted for the 2015 Short Story Day competition and anthologized in *Water: New Short Fiction From Africa*. His other short stories have been published in *Ake Review, Matatu, and The Price and Other Stories from Sierra Leone*. His research interests and scholarly publications include articles and book chapters on African trauma fiction, Afro diasporic literatures, and Sierra Leonean literature. Hollist is a 2017 Fulbright scholar and the 2014-2015 recipient of the Louise Loy Hunter Award, which is given annually by its previous recipients to a UT professor for excellence in teaching and cumulative contributions in service and scholarship.

Nine

A Life of Solitude

KHANU AND HIS 18-YEAR-OLD DAUGHTER BIANCA WATCHED the emergency-room doctor walk away after he delivered the news that Tamara, their wife and mother, was not only brain dead but was also carrying a three-week old fetus. They had discovered the pregnancy by chance. But because sometimes they cannot tell a viable one from a miscarriage, they wanted permission to run a transvaginal ultrasound to be sure. More than likely, the doctor had emphasized, lack of oxygen would have compromised the fetus, and it might be born with severe deformities. Depending on what the ultrasound shows, Father and daughter will have to decide whether they want to save the pregnancy, but they should know that keeping Tamara on the respirator would be costly for them and the hospital. Personnel from religious and social services were available to support them.

Father and daughter agreed to the test and flopped into the hardened plastic chairs of the waiting room, spent like chewed sugarcane pulp. Bianca sidled up to Khanu, the child soldier born to an abducted teen mom in an olive-green jungle. He did not remember much of his childhood in the battlefield, but as he sat in the clean, well-lit hospital, he recognized that the excitement now surging through him was the same he felt as an eight-year-old pointing his gun at his pleading victims and pulling the trigger, exerting revenge on a world that had left him, unwanted.

But that was a lifetime ago. Peacekeeping forces had rescued the boy from the combat zone, put him through rehabilitation, taught him a trade, and sent him to America as part of a youth delegation to the UN General Assembly to give firsthand accounts about the tribulations of being a child soldier.

Khanu was not, could not be, a designated speaker. Like the girls whose limbs had been amputated, he had been included in the group so the world could see the physical devastation of the Sierra Leonean war. His tongue had been sliced when he dared to tell his commander that he no longer wanted to be a soldier. The wound had healed him into silence, a world of solitude.

The day before he was supposed to return to Sierra Leone, Khanu slithered into the shadowy world of New York's undocumented immigrants. Years later, as a grown man in his thirties who could barely sign his name, he had married Tamara, twenty years his senior, from an old-money Alabama family. They lived in an upscale Birmingham community. His neighbors knew him as the quiet family man.

Into this father's chest, Bianca sank her head. She heard the rhythmic thump-thump of his heartbeat and felt his turmoil in his muscle twitches and the acidic smell of his sighs. She tightened her embrace as if to absorb his unrest. The gesture was futile, for the fuel stoking his inner strife came not from the grief of his brain-dead wife but from his inability to solve the arithmetic of her three-week-old pregnancy, minus a month of sexless marriage, times eighteen years of a vasectomy.

"We *cannot* take her off the ventilator!" Bianca spoke into Khanu's chest. She was a plainspoken child that never minced words. Khanu disliked this quality about his daughter, imprisoned as he was in silence.

Oh, yes, we can! Easily. I will cock my finger as if I was pulling a trigger and flick the ventilator off.

Bianca adjusted her head on her father's chest. "At least the child would be Mama's legacy."

And mine would be the trailing smell of disgrace. Turning the ventilator off is easy. Real justice should be slow and painful, like stoning her in the middle of a mall.

"I would have another brother, this time by the same parents."

Not wanting more children was the reason your mother said I should do the vasectomy. And I agreed. I had to. I wanted to become legal.

"I will help you raise the child. I am old enough. We have the money!"

We do not and have not for a while now. We might have to move out of the house. Your Grandpa's business is going bust, because of your clueless uncles and aunts. Your mom does not see that, but she tells me to buck up and get a better-paying job. Still, I did not cheat on her. I wonder whose child she is carrying.

Bianca raised her head from Khanu's chest. His breathing had quickened. The acidic smell had sharpened. She saw that he was awake, staring into the distance. She rubbed his chest in slow circular motions until she broke his stare and slowed his breathing. Then she nestled her head back on his chest. They sat in silence for a few minutes until she sighed: "And this was by far my best family reunion."

***

Khanu disliked the annual gathering—the papal deference to Big Nana, the surviving matriarch, and the obligation to listen, again, to the evolving epic about her husband, the benevolent, entrepreneurial patriarch and his struggles against racism. Khanu disliked, even more, the bland attempts by mediocre aunts, uncles, sisters, and brothers at pumping themselves up with their tales about projects that almost became mega-million dollar breakthroughs, but for the people determined not to let them succeed. He hated most the catalog of children--this boy and that girl born to unknown, absent, and shadowy hes and shes. Mostly, therefore, he stayed away from the rowdy centers of chatter and gluttony, preferring to sit with kindred spirits—the man in the wheelchair, the autistic boy, and the withdrawn child.

Still, he had vaguely looked forward to the reunion that had ended earlier that morning because Bianca had stumbled on her half-brother, Trekhan, on a Friends of Sierra Leone Facebook page. He had the same last name and looked like

Khanu. A few questions and likes later, the strangers agreed they *had* to be family if they were not half-siblings. Bianca showed her father the boy's photo.

She was a black Ameriasian woman, he signed to her. That's what they call children fathered by black American soldiers during the Vietnam War. He had dated her for a few months when he first came to America. She never told him she had a child for him.

Just a fling, he had flailed in front of Tamara. Nothing serious. They were both unwanted war babies. He was young, alone, immature, and he needed a place to stay. Come to think of it, she took advantage of him. Definitely unfair of her not to tell him about the boy.

"Your son," Tamara corrected. Children have no control over the circumstances of their birth," she continued. "The reunion would be a great place for all of us to get to know one another. Ideal for *us*," her pointer finger flickered between her and Khanu, "to figure out our future." He knew she wanted him to agree, to say something, but he locked up his thoughts.

The reunion went two-thirds well. Bianca and Trekhan shared tidbits about each other, their families, and their parents' birth countries. They giggled at or brushed away offbeat comments about his hair, nose, and complexion: "Hey Jackie Chan, you speak Chinese?" a man steadying himself on the arm of his female partner had yelled out as they passed by. "They speak Mandarin in China, motherfucker!" She yanked him away.

Tamara was ready to adopt Trekhan the moment she met him. Minutes into their first meeting, she asked for his mother's cell phone number and sent her a text message inviting them to Birmingham to celebrate Thanksgiving. Maybe, a son would pull Khanu out of his brooding she had justified the invitation to herself.

Khanu and Trekhan did not talk until dusk had settled on the first day, and then only because Bianca had dragged the son to meet the father who was sitting alone in the back yard.

She placed a chair in front of her dad and pushed Trekhan into it, and translated Khanu's questions. Trekhan answered them like a candidate who had made up his mind that he did not want the job at first sight of the interviewer.

"Yes, she is well. She sends her greetings. Soccer. In high school and at the University of Florida. Go Gators!" he chanted and brought his extended right arm down to meet his outstretched left. "That's the Gator chomp. It mimics the bite of an alligator. We use it to cheer our university teams, like how other fans clap for their teams. Summa cum Laude in biogenetic engineering and artificial intelligence. To make bionic people. You know, pacemakers, artificial limbs, and sex change. We are well on our way right now. I want to take hybridity to the next level. It makes sense to me. I am neither Asian nor African."

The reunion did not make father and son friends or heal the husband and wife's marital problems, but father, mother, and daughter left Pensacola, Florida, feeling hopeful about new beginnings. Gaiety and possibility filled the return car ride to Birmingham like lithium balloons on their way to a child's birthday celebration.

***

"What happened, Dad?" Bianca spoke into her father's chest. "Did you fall asleep?"

No, I went without sleep and food for three days as a child in the forest. I was awake, fully alert. Your mother had gone to sleep, her head and shoulders resting between the seat's headrest and the car window. You were slouched in the back. Couldn't tell if you were asleep or on your phone. I saw the sign "Birmingham 20" flash by. I looked over at your mother and saw her porky backside bulging out of her shorts. I don't know what happened. It had been months since I had been excited at seeing her. I reached out and stroked her back upper thighs with my fingers. She did not respond. I glanced at the rearview mirror to make sure you could not see my hand and reached out again. It would have been only a second or two, but when I turned my head back to the road, the wheels of the 18-wheeler clawed at the driver's side window. I swerved and lost control.

"Dad, you are not answering my questions." Bianca pulled back from her embrace and looked into Khanu's empty stare. "You want to take Mom off the ventilator?"

Khanu flinched before he regained full consciousness of his surroundings. Bianca saw the hesitation as confirmation of his intent.

"No, no, Dad. That will be murder. Double homicide."

But... but... she is brain-dead. The child will be deformed. The care, the costs! No matter what social services they say she is entitled to, the anesthesiologist, surgeon, and hospital will still bill me.

Bianca stormed off.

Khanu did not chase after Bianca. That was behavior for foolish Europeans and Americans who ceded their parental authority to mouthy, self-important children. She had marched off; she would have to march right back to him. He was not mad at her. How could a child, or anyone for that matter, know how he felt. He had not planned or wished for the way things had turned out. Now, he felt as if he had control over his life again. For a short time as a boy soldier in the olive-green forest, he had known what it felt like to be free of the needs of others, but he had lost that sense of liberty in the civilian world. Tamara's insurance policy will help him regain power.

No, he would not let them saddle him with caring for a deformed child. He had lived and known isolation and not belonging. He would not confer them on this child, even if it were not his. Therefore, he would tell them to turn off the ventilator. The last few oxygen molecules would trickle through it, but many would not. Tamara's chest wall would rise and fall one last time. The child would be spared his life of solitude.

Khanu saw them walking toward him, Bianca crying, held up by the emergency-room doctor and another woman. Anger flushed through his veins. He knew what was coming. She had reported him, and he was about to hear the riot act about not being an understanding, supporting parent.

They eased Bianca into the seat next to him, and she immediately clutched her father.

"I am sorry to tell you that neither your wife nor the fetus made it," the doctor said.

Bianca burst into a wail, and Khanu immediately clasped his daughter and broke down in tears.

Ten

The First-Place Poem Defense

THE TAXI SETS ME DOWN ON THE tree-lined street in front of one of New York's 19th-century brownstones. I compare the address written on the court order with the one on the building. They match. I climb up the steps to a black lacquered door and scan the engraved acrylic directory until I find her name: Jane Silverman, Clinical Psychology, Suite 101—just my luck to get a beginner. My resentment surges to my throat. I am *not* crazy, but the judge, in his haughty Ivy League accent, had looked at me right in the *ojukokoro* and said, "There's no doubt Ms. Mahene that you assaulted and severely injured your boyfriend. Ordinarily, I would be sentencing you, but something is wrong if your only defense is a poem for which you won first-place as a schoolgirl in Sira Leonie."

Sierra Leone, I hold my sneer. The judge shakes his head.

"I am ordering a full psychological evaluation. You either don't understand the gravity of your situation, or there's a cultural block somewhere we have to break through." He had slammed his mantel on the bench and had walked out.

Right, and now a white Jewish woman from Brooklyn will understand a village girl from Mogbwemo, Sierra Leone!

I turn the knob and enter suite 101. The door opens easily into a square waiting room. I walk up to the frosted sliding-glass window of the reception area and tap. No one answers. Obviously, Ms. Janie is not getting enough business to afford a receptionist. In a city of ten million, there surely ought to be enough nut jobs to keep all the city's shrinks busy. Clearly, the court-appointed ones must be young and incompetent, like my clueless public defender. And whether I go to jail or not depends on how Ms. Janie evaluates me. Does she even know that mental health is cultural? That, for example, poor kids in my country don't suffer from bulimia or anorexia. Do you know why? Because when you are hungry all day, vomiting food you've eaten is a freaking luxury! Same way, when an older man is messing with your child, you crack his skull, because 911 and social workers are not options.

I am angry now. I bang on the frosted sliding window. The glass shakes between the grooves. I cough loudly, once, twice. Nothing. I step back and survey the room. Only four chairs--confirmation Ms. Janie is not a successful shrink. Two of the chairs are on the left as you enter the waiting room. Against the adjacent wall, next to the door that leads into the consultation area, are the other two. Above them, side-by-side ads tout the benefits of Prozac, Paxil, Effexor, and Zoloft. On top of the ads is a dot-matrix printout, signed by Ms. Janie, that reads, "Don't let drug companies medicalize normal human experiences."

Hm! I like that. Ms. Janie may not be so bad after all. She is not likely to give me drugs that would make me loopy. I pick up *The Atlantic* from the center table. Ms. Janie must be left-leaning, probably nearer fifty than forty, grey-haired, overweight, and never married. No, married once, perhaps twice, but now divorced. Two children who have already left home, except that the eldest boy is undisciplined and trying to recover from the considerable college debt he has accrued without earning a degree. He wants to live with Ms. Janie, who refuses to allow him back into her home. She calls it tough love to teach him how to manage his money and be independent. But she also wants to keep him out of the house to assure she has the privacy for the occasional night of lurid sex. Of course, Ms. Janie owns a German shepherd she treats like a prince, visits museums, attends concerts, and donates to Greenpeace. And my fate is in the hands of this woman?

I fling the magazine onto the table, stand up, and stare at her framed certifications and degrees: A Bachelor's in psychology from Temple, a Ph.D. from New York University, and a license from New York State in 2005. I am calculating how long she has been practicing when the door into the consultation area opens.

"Mahin?"

"Mah-hay-ni."

"Am sorry, Maheyknee. My name is Dr. Silverman. How are you today?"

"I am fine, Dr. Sealvamin."

She is thinner and worldlier looking than I had imagined. More in her mid to late thirties. Dresses young. Underneath her white coat, she is wearing a deep V-neck, animal-print stretch gathered at the front by a hard dark brown, bone circle rim. Her skin is smooth. No lines or wrinkles. Her eyes are wide apart with makeup in the outer corners. She is wearing rimless black Gucci glasses and a wedding ring. A neat ballerina bun holds up her dark-brown hair at the back of her head. She is mature, intelligent-looking. Younger than me, but not by much o. I can see myself liking Ms. Janie, but my job is to make her believe me.

I walk into her office, and the sun splashes all over me like paint in a kiddie television game show. I shade my eyes.

"Two much light?" Ms. Janie scuttles over to the square bay windows with the heavy black and gold fabric curtains. Simultaneously, she reaches behind both curtains and pulls together the voile sheer. The intensity of the light fades into a soft hue.

"Please sit down," Ms. Janie points to a tweedy, wingback armchair. I sink into the chair, but immediately pull myself up and scoot to the front. I have to be alert. My freedom depends on what I say to Ms. Janie.

She sits in a leatherback chair with an upholstered seat section on top of which is a cushion. She towers over me. She opens my folder—the space in which my life experiences will be summarized into bullet points on a personality disorder scale—pulls out some papers and clicks her pencil but writes only a few words before the lead breaks. She pushes down on the knob and resumes her notations. The lead breaks again. She repeats this routine several times.

Use a bloody pen!

She confirms my name, address, social security number, and asks if I eat and sleep well and some other questions to test if I am crazy: do I feel lonely or have thoughts of killing myself. Suicide is cultural, ma'am. A real African does not commit suicide. Still, I answer her questions, but I am not really listening. I am looking at the large walnut desk and the ceiling-high bookcases of the same wood. I want to swivel and look at the rest of the office, but her questions intrude.

"Do you take any medications?"

"Yes."

"Name and dose?"

Damn! If you had a receptionist, I would have provided this information in triplicate!

"Verapamil."

"Dose?"

"I can't remember."

I don't like her questions, but I loved her firm, soft voice.

"Did they explain how this works?"

"Sort of. The judge said I must come and see you." I offered Ms. Janie the court order. She ignored it and pressed on.

"Once a month, I do pro-bono, that's free, work for ...."

That's right, Ms. Janie, explain what pro-bono means. I am black and need a court-appointed shrink, so I must be poor and uneducated. Okay, I am broke, but I have a degree from Strayer University, thank you! Okay, Ms. Janie. I am not as educated as you are, but I know what pro bono means, girlfriend. Yes, I am a fan of Sonny but not Cher!

People say I am funny. A smile sweeps across my face.

"I mostly work with abused women," Ms. Janie brushes off my amusement. "But I understand your case is different."

"Yeah, I am the abuser."

"Well, why don't you tell me what happened?"

"Read the poem. I say it all in there. That's my defense."

"I have read it. But you wrote the poem a long time ago. I want you to tell me what happened between your boyfriend and your daughter a few months ago."

"She is lying on the cold, white sheet--thin, naked, silent, still, her left hand flung back by the side of her head like the bone had been pulled out of its socket. She covers her eyes with her right forearm and turns her head to the side, away from his gaze, his rusty breath, him."

"You say she was naked?" Ms. Janie asks

"Yes."

"But the police report says she and your boyfriend were fully clothed when they got there. She says your boyfriend was helping her with a project."

"What do you expect her to say? He has brainwashed her."

"What makes you say that?"

"Because that's what they do. Older men gain their victim's confidence by helping with a project, don't they?"

Janie writes something into my summary.

"So, what happened next?"

"She trembles as he climbs onto the bed, engorged with excitement, his breath hot. His fingers rake her smooth, firm, and flat stomach; he shovels her small and pointy nipples into his mouth. Cockroaches and termites scramble through her."

"I see the picture of your daughter. She does not look small and pointy?"

"I am telling you what I saw."

"That's fine. You say your daughter felt like cockroaches were running through her body."

"Scrambling, crawling."

"How do you know that?"

"Goodness gracious. Have you ever disturbed an insect mound or disturbed a nest? Do you know how that takes away the creatures' sense of safety and comfort? She covers her eyes, has muscle spasms. Her legs twitch I know by her body language, gad dammit! She is a little girl. What could she do?"

"But she is over eighteen."

"Do you have children?"

"One boy, one girl."

"Do they ever stop being your children?"

"No."

"Well, then."

"But I stopped thinking about them as a little boy and girl once they turned eighteen."

"Well, where I come from, a child is always a child, no matter how old they are."

"Okay, let's agree to disagree. You describe what your daughter feels. How do you know what she feels?"

"I could feel. Can you not feel your kids' pain? Do you have to experience it to feel?"

Ms. Janie does not answer. I can see she is thinking, probably about her son. I realize I have her attention, so I press on. "I felt my people's pain when they learned the government had given away their land, even though I was only a little girl. Is that crazy?"

Ms. Janie scribbles furiously on the pad. I stop talking.

"Your people?"

"Yes, you should have read my poem? That is my defense."

"I see. We will get to the poem soon. If you saw what was happening, why did you not shout and call for help?"

"And wait till fire-rescue comes? I clocked him on his gad dam head. Maybe I should have killed him?"

"Okay, okay. You could feel your daughter's pain. What happened next?"

"She trembles, tries to cover herself, but he is touching her, ploughing through the tuft of hair in her armpit and the other clump between her thighs. They snap together, cemented by a thin layer of sweat. He jams his right knee into her left thigh. The electric pain jolts them apart. She swings her right leg across her body and blocks his advances with the back of her thigh. He pulls and claws; she slithers and twists. He pants and stops; she exhales. He looks over to the corner of the room, mutters, and growls to them."

"And while all this is happening, you still did nothing?"

"I am giving you a play-by-play. At that time, it happened so fast."

"But you seem to remember precise details as if you were the one experiencing them."

"I was there, remember."

"I would have shouted, screamed, found some way to let them know I was watching. Surely that would have made him stop."

"What world do you come from? I could not do anything because my aunties walk over to us. One grabs my wrists and yanks my arms parallel to my ears. The other grabs my ankles and pulls them apart. I must have blacked out. The next thing I remember is hearing his frog-in-heat voice in my ear."

"The ones before you groaned, complained that it hurt, screamed, and cried. You, little one, you have the heart of a leopard. You accepted me, as would a mother of ten! But wait-o. Not even a whimper. Did I spend thousands of Leones, rebuilt your father's home only to be mocked, to stare at a white sheet?"

I am sure he is about to beat me when he notices the crimson array. "Aaa," he moans. "It was the first of many that night and each made me cry."

I open my eyes to see Janie writing frantically into the folder.

"Are you okay?"

I nod and mumble something like a yes, but my brain is full of cobwebs.

We stare at each other for a couple of minutes. Ms. Janie is looking at me as if she does not quite know what to make of my story.

"You switched voice, pronoun."

"And?"
"You were describing something that happened to you."
I sniff and look away.
Ms. Janie stands up and leaves the office. A minute later, she returns with two cups of water in those white Styrofoam cups.
"Tell me about the poem. Why did you write it?"
"To protest the mining companies. They were destroying our Land. Flooding it, stealing our diamonds, profiting from them, and leaving us with nothing except sickness and death. It is a good poem. I didn't think I would win, but I did."
"Do you want to read it?"
"No."
"Try."
She held out two sheets of photocopied paper. The first page read:
> This First-Place Poem is awarded in Absentia to Mahene Gamanga
> Mogbwemo Town Poetry Competition 1989

On the second page was the poem. I read it.

Land that We Love
They, the faces in white shirts and khaki shorts,
Shaved, felled, and gorged her.
They trampled, flooded, and dammed her.
They broke into her sacred bush
The ancient riverbed
Dredged and scooped her,
Morning, noon, and night, till
She screamed and bled the ores and devil stones.
"For progress and development," they chimed.
Cracked and crusted now,
Unfit to nourish or to be re-nourished
She sits used and abused, land that we love(d).

"It's a beautiful poem. Why did you not go to receive your prize in person?"

"We had left Mogbwemo. One of my classmates collected and brought it to me."

"So, when did you write it?"

"The morning after the wedding."

"Which wedding?"

I do not answer. She's the shrink. Let her figure it out.

"Yours?"

I do not answer, but the question is rhetorical.

Ms. Janie had turned her attention to her notes and was scribbling again. But this writing was different. I could clearly see the letters, each well-formed, the spaces between them equal. Together, they merged into whole words that proceeded logically, one after another into sentences and then into a paragraph, an organic whole, a first-place prose poem, a cultured picture for the judge.

"You will be fine," Ms. Janie said to me after she stopped writing, her eyes ablaze with empathy.

I inhaled and smiled.

Naana Banyiwa Horne

Naana Banyiwa Horne, Ph.D. (Nana Ansomaa III) is a retired Professor of English, Africana Studies and Gender Studies. Dr. Horne has held teaching positions in universities in Ghana and the United States and has published scholarly as well as creative works. She has published "Payback," a short story in *Payback and Other Stories*, edited by Tomi Adeaga and Sarah Udoh-Grossfurthner, two collections of poetry and two more awaiting publication. Horne is currently working on a book on Gender in Ghanaian Literature and a collection of short stories. A Twidan Abusua Gyasi Hemmaa of Akwamufie, her life and 2010 enstool-ment at Akwamufie are documented in the film *Chosen*, by the preeminent African documentary filmmaker, Jean-Marie Teno.

Eleven

Miimi Is Being Bad Again

MY NAME IS MIIMI. I HAVE A brother and a sister. First, there is the boy, Fiifi; then myself, and then Dinni. People have said "the middle child" so much when they mean me, I have accepted *that* as my special name.

I have always wanted lots of brothers and sisters, just like Mmaa and Mmpa. Large families are lots of fun. You have a whole lot of people to play with and also to pick up after yourselves. I know my brother Fiifi and my baby sister Dinni feel the same way.

Do you believe every time we tell Mmaa to have another boy and girl together, she tells us we are crazy? Can you believe that coming from someone who comes from a big family herself? She loves to let us know her Mama and her Papa had four girls and five boys, and she is the oldest and *THE BOSS* of everybody. I too want to be *THE BOSS*. Just like Mmaa.

I know you are thinking, "How can she be a real boss over only two people? And she's not even the first born?" I don't mind that I am not the first born, because everybody thinks I am. *I am* the biggest one of us three.

No! Fiifi can't be *THE BOSS*. He's a cry-baby. He whines too much. He's the only boy, and there are two of us girls. So, GIRLS RULE! To be a real boss, though, I need many more people to boss. That's why I need Mmaa to give me lots of sisters and brothers.

Mmpa, too, comes from a large family. They're eleven altogether. He has way more brothers and sisters than Mmaa. We've lots of aunties and uncles in both Ghana and Miami. As for cousins we've so many; many more than all our friends. I believe we've the most cousins in the whole wide world.

All Mmpa's brothers and sisters we know, because they also live in Miami. But we only hear of Mmaa's father and her brothers and sisters. We haven't seen any of them, because they live in Accra, Ghana. Mmaa loves to talk about her family in Ghana, especially Daddy, our grandpa, and Auntie Adjowa, the one she calls her bestest buddy that none of us knows. We know only Auntie Kai. She lives in Virginia, and she visits us in Miami, or we go to see her and our three cousins in Springfield. They're all boys, so they play mainly with Fiifi. They barely play with Dinni and me. But we don't mind too much, because Auntie Kai loves to spoil us girls. She doesn't have any girls herself.

Auntie Kai's real name is Maame Esi Kaiko, but Mmaa calls her Kai. Mmaa is older than Auntie Kai, but our auntie is bigger and taller. She's always telling people she's Mmaa's Big Aunt. Whenever she says that, Mmaa turns to look at us and points at her, "Auntie Kai! She's the clown of the family." We all laugh, including Auntie Kai herself.

I know both Mmaa and Mmpa had lots of fun growing up. What with so many brothers and sisters to play with all the time and also to fight. True they had to share more and didn't have as much stuff as we do. But I don't mind sharing my stuff with people I like, because I can always play with them. And if I fight with one, I can always play with another one. And then, when we have to clean up or pick up or do something, *like we're made to do*, more people always pick up faster and get more time to play.

I have only Fiifi, and Dinni is to play with. She is the baby, so I can't even fight her. Not yet, anyway. She is the one who hits and scratches all of us. But, then, everybody tells me and Fiifi: "Oh, don't mind her; she's the baby." They don't want to hear that Dinni is bad.

I like to play with her and take care of her. But she hits and scratches me real hard sometimes. And she can scream hard too. She screams harder than anyone I know.

"Leeee me alone!" she's always screaming. Even if I try to

hit her just to teach her a lesson about being bad to me, she screams; then everybody tells me: "Be good to your baby sister."

Dinni's a lot of fun when she is not being bad, scratching and hitting. But I don't like not being able to hit her back when she hits and scratches me. If I don't hit her back, how will she learn she can't go around hitting people?

Two of Mmaa's sisters have come to visit us — Auntie Kai, and Auntie Adjowa, Mmaa's bestest buddy. She has come from Ghana with her two children to visit Auntie Kai and Mmaa. They flew into Washington, D.C. because Springfield, where Auntie Kai lives, is very close to D.C., the nation's capital, and to two international airports. And there is a lot to see in D.C. Auntie Kai didn't bring her boys this time, but we are very happy because she brought Auntie Adjowa and her children to Miami to visit with us.

Auntie Adjowa hasn't seen Mmaa in gazillion years. Mmaa left home a long time ago. So long ago that Mmaa doesn't even know Auntie Adjowa's children, Sedi and Fafa. My two aunties came with Sedi and Fafa.

Oh, were we all so happy, especially Mmaa. Sedi and Fafa are bigger than Fiifi, myself, and Dinni. Sedi's a boy, so Fiifi has someone to play with. And Fafa, a girl, is big enough to spoil Dinni and me. We've heard so much about them, and we're really happy! Especially they have come to visit, so we can get to play with them.

It's when Mmaa's sisters are visiting with us that we find out how much fun Mmaa can be. She definitely must have had a lot of fun growing up with so many brothers and sisters. Many times, she and her sisters act just plain silly. They're very funny. They don't talk about sensible things. They talk a lot; but they talk about funny stuff and laugh so much. I can't understand most of what they're talking about, because they speak one or the other language from Ghana. They often mix that up with a funny kind of English and then tease us. "We are not like you Americans who speak only one language—English," Mmaa will say. Then Auntie Kai will add, "And it's not even proper English." I don't need to understand what they are saying to know they are not being serious.

Aren't grown-ups supposed to act serious-like—the way Mmaa acts when she is by herself? She is always telling us, "Behave," and "Hurry up and do what you are supposed to do." But with her sisters here, she isn't telling us what to do too much. She's having too much fun herself to be bothered much by our silliness. And we're loving that very much.

Mmaa, Auntie Adjowa, and Auntie Kai are just like Fiifi, Dinni, and myself. They act silly and funny, calling each other funny names. They also imitate their Daddy, our grandpa, and the oldest of the boys, the one who's number three out of the nine of them. Auntie Kai actually comes after him. They say things that sound silly even to us kids, even if we do not understand what they are saying. The difference is that they don't fight like we do. They laugh all the time. They are all so happy. I don't remember seeing Mmaa so happy.

We're also very happy. We've our cousins from Ghana around to play with all the time. And there is our mother so happy she's quite fun to be around. And then there are our two aunties making Mmaa so happy and busy spoiling us too. I want life to be like this forever.

I'm sad. I'm very sad. Auntie Adjowa and her children are leaving. I want them to stay. I tell them it's all right for them to stay with us. We don't mind sharing our room with them. But Auntie Adjowa says they *have to go back*; and Mmaa also says the same thing.

It doesn't worry me that Auntie Kai is going back. We all like her, but we're not too unhappy that she has to leave. After all, she didn't bring her children with her. And I know we'll see her soon. It's easy to visit her. But Auntie Adjowa we may never see again. And that makes me very, very sad.

Auntie says they have to leave because they have a plane

to catch to get back to Ghana. And Mmaa says the same thing. I tell them I want to catch the plane too. I want to go with them to Ghana. That's when Mmaa tells me I can't get on the plane without a ticket, and I'll need gazillion money to get the ticket. Even when I pull out all the money I have in my piggybank, she tells me that's way too little to buy me a ticket.

I'm feeling so bad I want to cry. So, I go to our room and sit on the bed, playing with my favorite doll. That's when I realize I don't want to leave Mmaa and Mmpa and Fiifi and Dinni and all our toys and friends.

We all go outside to watch our aunties and cousins get into the car after hugging us. We continue to wave until their car disappears. After standing outside for a while, we go back inside. Fiifi and Dinni both start to cry. I call them "cry babies." Mmaa herself is sad. I'm sure she's crying silently like she does sometimes but pretends she isn't. When I ask her why her eyes are red and leaking water, she says something has fallen in her eye.

Following our aunties visiting us and leaving, I have become very sad. With our cousins gone, I have just Fiifi and Dinni. I want more than ever for Mmaa to have more children.

We are all happy again. Mmaa's stomach is getting big. She tells us we're going to have another brother *or* sister. "A brother *and* a sister," we scream with joy. "We want a brother and a sister." We tell Mmaa so. If she gives us a brother and a sister together every time she has a baby, I will have gazillion sisters, and Fiifi can have a few brothers so he doesn't feel left out.

Everybody's happy that Mmaa's stomach is growing. But we're happiest of all. We love to rub our hands on her stomach to hug our babies who are growing in there. Fiifi wants a little brother. And I want another sister. Mmaa likes to make us happy. I know she will have another sister for me and a brother for Fiifi. Her friends always want to hug her too and put their hands on her stomach as if they are listening to our babies talking.

"Mmaa, are our babies ready to come out of your stomach yet?"

"No, Miimi, I keep telling you there's only one baby in my stomach and it will be a long time before the baby is ready to come out of me."

"But we asked for a brother and a sister. And, Mmaa, you love us both, right? So, please give Fiifi a brother, and give me another sister."

"But Miimi, most mothers have only one child whenever they give birth. Fiifi was born alone. So were you, and so was Dinni."

"Well, if there's only one baby in your stomach, then I want a girl. A girl's more fun to play with. And my brother Fiifi, he whines a lot. I don't want any more whinos. But I also want Fiifi to be happy, so he can have a little brother just like I have a little sister, Dinni."

"Oh, Miimi, that's very sweet of you.

"Group hugs, Mmaa."

Mmaa has her arms wide and all three of us move close to her and put our ears to her stomach and our arms around her; then she hugs us tight.

Mmaa has started going to see the baby-doctor. We love to go with Mmaa, so we can dance with our babies. There's no way Mmaa'll not give us another girl and boy. She loves us so much she'll give me a girl and Fiifi a boy.

It's at the doctor's office that we hear our babies dance when the doctor puts on Mmaa's stomach that little round thing with gooey stuff on it and the name that's too long and hard to say. Then we all dance together to the music coming from our babies in Mmaa's stomach. We love that time of Mmaa's visits to the doctor.

We try to dance with our babies in Mmaa's stomach when we go to dance class with her. But we don't hear any music coming from our babies then. We only have the music coming from the drums and other instruments. So, we always beg to go with her to dance during her doctor's visits.

Even the doctor loves it when we dance to the music coming from Mmaa's stomach. He tells us we dance well and it's good that we like to make our baby happy by dancing. We look forward so much to these visits, but it takes a long time before Mmaa goes to see the doctor again.

Whenever we talk about our babies, Mmaa tries to tell us we are having only one baby, and we don't like to hear that. And when we ask to go with her to the doctor's office, so we can dance to the drum music from our babies, she likes to say it is the baby's heartbeat we are hearing and not the baby dancing. But we know better. What Mmaa likes to call the baby's heartbeat sounds just like the drums to which we dance. It goes *dum, dum-dum, dum-dum, dum-dum;* and then *du-dum, du-dum, du-dum, du-dum.*

We prefer the drum-sounds coming from our babies in the doctor's office. They are faster, and we can dance with our babies. We can dance real fast and have lots of fun. Oh, we look forward to that so much. And even the doctor loves our dancing with our babies. He laughs too when Mmaa says, "They are so crazy."

One day, we wake up and Mmaa and Mmpa are gone. Uncle James is in the house with us. He tells us Mmpa and Mmaa have gone to the hospital, and that he will take us to Auntie's on his way to work. Auntie is Grandma's big sister. She's home a lot, so she keeps us sometimes when Mmaa and Mmpa have to go and Grandma is at work, and we can't go to school. And there is always someone at Auntie's.

We love when Cousin Drew is home, because he lets us go into his room and watch TV. We watch what he is watching. We get to watch shows Mmaa and Mmpa don't let us watch. And we love that. Even though I miss Mmaa and Mmpa, I'm happy because I know soon our babies will be here.

We wait at Auntie's for Mmpa to come back and get us. I'm eager to go see Mmaa and our new babies. It takes a long time for Mmpa to come. And when he shows up, he looks very tired. We're all so excited, asking about our babies and asking for him to take us to the hospital to see them. But he looks very tired and doesn't seem too happy.

When he tells us we have a baby sister, I start jumping and screaming: "I win; GIRL'S RULE." I don't even mind Mmpa telling me to be quiet. I am too happy to completely shut up. I want a girl if we can't have both a girl and a boy. I start to sing: "We have a girl. We have a girl." Mmpa gives me the BEHAVE look.

"Do we have a baby brother too?" Fiifi asks. His face grows so long when Mmpa says: "No, just a baby sister." "No-o-o-o! That is not fair! It *is* not fair!" Fiifi keeps whining. So, I stick my tongue out at him and scream. "Whino!" Again, Mmpa tells me, "Cut that out. Get your stuff. It's time to go."

When we leave Auntie's, I tell Mmpa we want to go to the hospital to see Mmaa and the baby. But he takes us home and gets some clothes for us. Then he takes us to Grandma's.

"I don't want to stay at Grandma's," I say. I want to go with Mmpa to the hospital.

Mmpa stays and talks with Grandma a little bit. We don't hear what they're talking about, because they go into her bedroom and shut the door. When they come out, Mmpa goes to the kitchen, dishes out some food for us and we sit down at the table and eat. After helping us to clean up, he sits down to watch the news, but he is soon snoring. He gets up suddenly and tells grandma he is going back to the hospital and will see us in the morning.

Normally, we're happy to spend weekends at Grandma's because we can play with our cousins who are with her at the time. But this time, I start to cry because I really want to go with Mmpa to the hospital to see Mmaa and our new baby. Dinni and Fiifi also start crying, but Mmpa leaves us anyway. He comes back in the morning just before Grandma has to leave for work. He helps us clean up, put our clothes on, and eat. When we leave, I expect him to take us to the hospital to see Mmaa and the baby; but he takes us to Auntie's.

"What about the hospital? Can we go see Mmaa and our baby sister?" I ask. But Mmpa says, "Later, I will go to the office and then come to Auntie's to pick you up and take you to the hospital." We don't like it, but we agree to be good at Auntie's.

In the evening Mmpa picks us up again from Auntie's and takes us to Grandma's. He tells us we will have to spend the night again, because he has to go back to the hospital. This time, I really want to see Mmaa and the baby and I start to tell Mmpa so. But his face looks so worried I decide not to fuss. Even Fiifi doesn't whine, and Dinni cries only a little bit.

I remember when Mmaa had Dinni at the hospital. Mmpa took us to see them. And we know Mmaa is at the same hospital. I wonder why he isn't taking us this time. And every time I start to ask him, he looks so worried I decide to wait. We keep going to Auntie's in the daytime and sleeping at Grandma's for what seems like forever.

Then one afternoon Mmpa comes early to Auntie's to get us. We get in the car and he takes us home. We get to the house and Mmaa is already home. We are happy to see her, and eagerly ask: "Where are our babies?" She starts to cry.

It seems like she's been crying even before we came home. It is Mmpa who tells us, "Your baby sister is still in the hospital. She has to stay there for some time." Fiifi and I both say together, "But we want our sister home now." Mmpa tells us, "Don't worry. She will come home. Please! Both of you!"

We don't like our baby being in the hospital, so I tell Mmaa, "We want our baby. We don't like to leave her in the hospital. Mmaa, can you bring our baby home?" That makes Mmaa cry even more. So, we stop asking to have our baby. Since I don't like to see Mmaa cry, I decide to say it only in my head. "I want my baby home! I want my baby home." But even that I have had to stop because it seems like Mmaa can hear me, for she is crying even more. Fiifi says in a very soft voice, "Mmaa, don't worry, okay? Our baby sister will come home soon."

Mmaa goes to the hospital every day and spends almost all her time there. We have to go to Auntie's and grandma's a lot. But then one day, when Mmpa brings us home from Auntie's, we find Mmaa sitting in the sofa with our baby in her arms, wrapped in a baby blanket.

We get very excited and all three of us start to rush to Mmaa and our baby. But Mmpa goes "shhhh" and tells us we have to wait for him to take us one by one to hug our baby. He takes Dinni first. But as soon as she sees our baby in Mmaa's arms, she starts to throw up. She throws up on the baby, but Mmaa moves her arms very fast to her side and the throw-up falls on her feet. I screech, "Oooh! That's gross." I am thinking Mmaa or Mmpa will scream at me to behave. They don't.

Mmpa takes our baby from Mmaa, and she picks Dinni up and holds her in her arms the way she was holding the baby. She wipes Dinni's face and rocks her like our new baby. Dinni falls asleep quickly and Mmaa takes her to their bedroom and lays her down on their bed.

As soon as Mmaa gets off the sofa, Mmpa sits down still holding our baby in his arms. So me and Fiifi rush to him to see our baby. "Give me my baby. I want to hold my baby," I say. But he tells me "shhhh!" I look at the baby. But I see only one side of her face. She looks tiny. She is quiet, and her eyes are closed. I walk away and hope Fiifi will also come so we can look for something fun to do. But he stands by Mmpa and the baby, just looking at her.

Mmaa comes from the room and sits back down on the sofa. Mmpa hands her the baby and I follow him into the kitchen to help get us drinks and snacks. Fiifi does not want any snack. He stands quietly by Mmaa and the baby for a while. Then he says in a very sad voice: "Mmaa, why does our baby look like Beast in *Beauty and the Beast*? What is wrong with her face … her mouth?"

Mmaa says nothing for a long while. Finally, she calls me

to come and stand with Fiifi. She turns the baby so she is lying on her back in her lap and facing us. Mmaa pulls Fiifi and I close. She wraps her arms around us and then says in a very soft voice: "Mimi and Fiifi, your baby sister, Nana Araba, is sick. She has what is called a birth defect. She has a tear, a cleft, in her lip and all the way into her palate. She has what is called a cleft lip and palate. It is because she is sick that I stayed in the hospital with her for so long."

"Mmaa, is she going to die? I don't want her to die."

"Can we fix her up? We can put Band-Aid on her mouth for her *awui* to go away."

When Mmaa starts to speak again, her voice sounds very sad. But she is not crying.

"Sorry guys, but Band-Aid will not fix her mouth. The doctors can fix her up, they say. But she will have to have a *lot* of surgery. A lot of surgeries... It will take a long time. But the doctors believe they can fix her up real good. Nana Araba will need lots of love and prayers."

"Mmaa, I know how to pray. I can say Amen. Can we pray for her now so she gets fixed?"

Daddy tells us all to hold hands and look at Nana Araba. He starts to pray and we all listen. Finally.

"In the name of the Father, and of the Son, and of the Holy Spirit. As it was in the beginning is now and ever shall be, world without end." And we all say together, "Amen."

Our baby is quiet most of the time. But she cries sometimes, especially when she wants food. And she likes to eat a lot, even though she doesn't suck breast milk like the three of us did when we were babies. Mmaa has to pump her milk and pour it into a bottle with a funny-looking nipple. She squeezes a few drops at a time in her mouth. Then we hear her swallowing very loud.

I am sad. I want to play with her. Have some fun with her. But Mmaa tells me she won't be able to play for a long, long time. I don't like that. I don't like it at all. I want to play with

Nana Araba. I want to show her to my friends. But Mmaa tells me I can't. She is busy with the baby all the time. She is no fun. I want our Mmaa back. The one we had when my aunties came to visit.

It is Tuesday. One week since the baby has been home. It is early in the morning, but we are all up and excited. It is the day for our baby's outdooring and naming ceremony. The ceremony was supposed to happen one week after our baby was born. But she has only been out of the hospital for a week.

Mmaa and Mmpa and all of us are dressed in white. Chief, Yeye, and two other grown-ups we know have come to our house for the event. They had brought food with them, and Mmpa has bought drinks and some candy and chips from the store. Four of our "cousins" have come with Chief and Yeye, so we have people to play with. We stay in our room with our cousins and play. These are not our cousins like Sedi and Fafa. But we call them our Miami cousins. Our families have become very close, and we do a lot of things together.

After a while, Yeye comes to the room to call us to come join the gathering. The ceremony is done and it is time to eat and have fun. Our baby Nana Araba is lying asleep on Auntie Dede. The baby has gone back to sleep, so we let her be and continue to have fun with our cousins.

We become sad when our cousins have to leave and ask if they can stay with us. But then Yeye tells us the baby needs rest so they have to leave. We are not happy about that. But then she tells us we get to go home with them for the rest of the day. *That* makes us happy.

One week following the naming of Nana Araba Sunkwa, Mmaa starts screaming shortly after feeding our baby. Mmpa comes out of the bedroom to find out what is wrong. Mmaa screams: "Call 911. Nana Araba has stopped breathing." Mmpa grabs a blanket and spreads it on the floor. He is still on the phone. And Mmaa lays our baby down on the blanket. She kneels beside her and then puts her mouth over the baby's mouth and blows air into her. She does this a few times, then she picks up our baby and sits down, breathing real deep. She tells Daddy to get her bag and the baby's bag ready.

When the ambulance pulls up and Mmaa and our baby get inside. It drives off making a loud noise. Fiifi and Dinni start to cry, but I don't cry. Our next door neighbor comes to take us to her house, so Mmpa can drive to the hospital where Mmaa and our baby have been taken.

"Our baby is going to the hospital to die."
"No-o-o-o! Don't say that. They will fix her up so she *will* be fine. Then she can play with us."

"No. She will die."
"Miimi, stop being bad."

Mmaa and Mmpa start going to the hospital again every day. And we start going to Auntie's and Grandma's again. Daddy will drop Mmaa off at the hospital and then drop us off at Auntie's on his way to work. On his way from work he picks Mmaa up from the hospital. Then they pick us up from Auntie's. Once we get home, they feed and bathe us, put our sleeping clothes on us, and then take us to Grandma's. They will both leave for the hospital. Most times, we are already sleeping by the time they pick us back up to come home.

This goes on for two weeks. But on Friday morning, Mmaa and Mmpa tell us we are all going to the beach. We start dancing because we are really happy to spend time with our parents having fun. But just when we are walking out the door, the phone rings and Daddy answers it. He whispers to Mmaa, "It is the hospital."

Mmaa immediately bursts out crying, sobbing uncontrollably. "*Ow Ewuradze!* Oh God. *Meba yi-o-o, Me ba yi!*" My child! Oh, my child!

Mmpa moves close to Mmaa and wraps his arms around her. Dinni runs to Mmaa crying. And Fiifi is standing there looking *shit-faced* at no one in particular. I walk up to him and say under my breath: "I told you they were taking our baby to the hospital to die."

Twelve

Reconnected Redefined

"THE TEST CAME OUT POSITIVE," DR. DAVIS said matter-of-factly. Mansa was sitting motionless, her face an impenetrable mask. Puzzled, the doctor resorted to stealing furtive glances at her, hoping for clues to how she was processing the news. But her mind was all the way back in Ghana, on her mother and her aunties back home.

"Muwuraba," she remembered them saying on her last trip home. "By all means pursue your education to the highest level you can. Nothing beats a woman who has her own children and a good job to provide for herself and her children. Of course, it is best if you have a good man who loves you and provides for you and your children. What child wouldn't choose jollof rice over plain rice any day if it is offered?"

These were the same aunties who had said when she announced her admission to her first university after graduating from high school, "Don't forget you are a Ghanaian woman; there are things that should be more important in a Ghanaian woman's life. After all, a degree cannot fetch you water to drink."

That seemed so long ago. The approval rate of these same aunties grew so high over the years that they started referring to her affectionately as "*Muwuraba*, My Lady," instead of plain old Mansa, or "*Ewuraba Katsina*; Iron Lady; Lady Jane Gray."

"Meba Mansa who floods my heart with joy. Don't you worry about a thing. One hand bathes the other. When it's your turn to have babies, I will be there for you. My most dear child, 'the one who feels for me,'" Mamaa used to say, whenever Mansa excelled in being her mother's 'very good daughter.'

At the point in her life when she needed mothering the most, Mansa had to be her own mother and mother to her babies. Mamaa died five years ago none of the aunties eager to babysit were available. She was in America while all those aunties were either taking care of their own daughters and grandchildren abroad or were far away in Ghana. The current pregnancy would make the fourth child she would be having while working on her doctoral dissertation.

At last, Mansa stopped exhuming those past promises that would never be realized. She rose from her seat, an enigmatic smile on her face. "No one back home can say *I* don't have my priorities right. Not anymore, Doctor. Thank you." She opened the door and closed it behind her.

Mansa Ansah left Ghana for America in 1979 to further her education in Literary Studies at the University of Florida (UF). She was assigned an apartment in the graduate student housing complex. Coming out around 10:00 p.m. for air on her first day in the complex, she bumped into another occupant, a six-three mahogany male who was also taking a break from studying.

"Hi, neighbor, welcome to Shuckt Village. This must be your first day here." He extended his hand. "I am DeJohn Jones. From Miami."

"Mansa Ansah. From Ghana. It must be a good omen to encounter a black male graduate student in this sea of whiteness."

"It is. There are definitely fewer than ten black students in the whole complex. I've been here, in this complex, for two years. But I've been at UF for five years. I used to live in an apartment not far from the campus."

"In the student ghetto," the two said in unison, laughing. They walked to where the walkway into the apartment complex connected to the street; and then they turned around and walked back. When they reached DeJohn's building, he told Mansa he would walk her home if she didn't mind stopping for him to check on his dinner in the oven. She accompanied him in. He got back, right on time to pull out a nicely browned sausage and a sizeable baked sweet potato. "I learned this trick from my Mama. All I have to do is to take out the sausage and potato, pull out the foil and dump it in the trash. It makes cleaning the pan very easy."

Here was a guy comfortably talking about kitchen tricks he had learned from his mother. "You seem definitely comfortable in the kitchen."

"I learned to cook early because I love to eat. Mama would leave home real early for work and return after seven. She had eleven of us. I am her third child and the first to be born in the city of Miami. I would wake up my younger siblings, feed them, then take them to school before making it to school myself."

"Wow, I'm impressed. My mother had nine children. Being the first born and my mother's helper, I loved shadowing her in the kitchen, wanting to know everything. That's how I learned to cook. Good a thing I did, because she died when I was fourteen, my first year at St. Mary's Secondary School. I took over running our household whenever I came home on break. When I graduated at the top of the honors program in English at the University of Cape Coast, I was appointed to teach in the English Department the year I graduated. I went back home and got my youngest sister who was in her teens, and my four youngest siblings, all boys, to live with me on the Cape Coast University campus. All those boys learned to cook and became great cooks."

DeJohn dished out two plates, each with half of the sausage, and half of the sweet potato, and two glasses of red cool-aid; and they ate. Then he walked Mansa to her apartment, helped her finish unpacking and said good night, promising to come by in the morning to walk with her to the campus, showing her the quickest way to her department.

This chance encounter between the two developed into a close friendship. A six-three mahogany male companion who knew his way around campus and the city of Gainesville was definitely a game-changer. Not only did DeJohn's presence dull those surges of lonesomeness that played havoc on foreign students; it shielded Mansa from the rampant assaults on women on campus and on city streets. The two studied hard on week days and partied on campus and in nightclubs in the city on weekends. DeJohn, being an avid chess player, taught Mansa to play his favorite game.

Within two years, Mansa had completed her course work, passed the qualifying exam, and submitted a proposal to explore "The Theme of Woman Being in Ama Ata Aidoo's Works" for her doctoral dissertation. Neither her topic nor her chosen advisor was approved under the guise that no one in the English Department could work with her on *that* topic. Dr. Mildred Anderson, the professor Mansa chose as her dissertation advisor, was an African American woman in the English department whose specialty was African and African Diaspora literature. Mansa had taken every class offered by her, Aidoo's works being among her most frequently offered classes.

Ironically, Mansa had chosen to attend UF after meeting Dr. Anderson at the University of Cape Coast on a trip to Ghana to interview Ama Ata Aidoo for a book project. Agonized by the blatantly racist underpinnings of the English Department's decision to approve neither her topic nor choice of dissertation advisor, Mansa opted for a Masters with Thesis in order to keep both her advisor and topic. Then, she went ahead to apply to the University of Wisconsin's Department of African Languages and Literature to pursue her doctorate while still working on her M. A. thesis.

Admitted to start at UW-Madison in the fall of 1982, Mansa encouraged DeJohn, who was also writing his thesis on "Case Mix Resource Allocation: Implications for Hospital Management Control," to accompany her to Madison. Working steadily on their theses during Mansa's first year in the African Languages and Literature program and returned to Gainesville, they were able to return to Gainesville in the summer to submit and defend their theses. Once done with their obligation to UF, the two headed to Miami, DeJohn's hometown, in the third week in July, to vacation.

On a beautiful Friday afternoon at Bill Baggs Cape Florida State Park in Key Biscayne, DeJohn and Mansa frolicked in the Atlantic Ocean close to the Lighthouse until sunset. Then with his left arm wrapped around her shoulder, and her right hand around his waist, they started to head back to the beach, moving leisurely and soaking in the spectacular sunset. About ten feet from the shore, DeJohn stopped and turned sideways slowly, causing Mansa to also turn sideways facing him. He brought his hand down from her shoulder and gently took hold of both her hands, pensively looking into her eyes but saying nothing for a long while. Just when she started to wonder what was up with him, he found his tongue.

Slowly, reflectively, he started speaking. "Mansa, I don't know how I will do this. But if you will let me, I will love to take care of you for the rest of my life." Taken totally by surprise, Mansa was silent for a long minute with a quizzical look on her face, wondering if she had heard what she thought she had. Slowly she lifted her face to look DeJohn directly in his eyes. He looked so forlorn she couldn't help but burst out laughing, realizing he had mistaken her slowness in responding for rejection. Once it sank into his head that Mansa was laughing her happy laugh and nodding her consent, he put his hands under her armpit, lifted her up to eyelevel, and started to twirl, the two of them laughing joyously. They stayed at the beach till sundown before returning to the house.

On the way back to the house, they talked about when and where they would like to get married. Miami would definitely be the venue, and the month would be June of the following year. After dinner, DeJohn informed Mama about his and Mansa's desire to return to Miami to get married in June. Mama was ecstatic; she began planning their wedding that night—calling family to tell them the good news and to assign each group specific dish(es) to contribute towards the wedding reception.

In mid-August, 1983, the lovebirds returned to Madison. Mansa geared up for her second year of studies in African and African Diaspora Orature and Literary Studies, and to teach the two classes she had been assigned—Introduction to African Studies and Introduction to Afro-American Studies. DeJohn picked up temporary jobs while looking for jobs commensurate with his education in Business Management and Administrative Sciences. Thankfully, in October, he was offered a position as Financial Economist at the Public Service Commission of Wisconsin.

In no time spring was upon them. The spring semester ended the first week in May. Once done with her obligations to her professors and her students, Mansa had lots of time to relax, gallivant some, and hang out with her two friends, Diana and Ndyanao. She also spent time in the library doing research and preparing for the next academic year. With DeJohn working full time he couldn't be away from work for more than three weeks.

Mansa and DeJohn left for Miami on Friday night of the third week in May to get married on Saturday, June 2nd, 1984. Diana from Chicago, a student in Law School at UW-Madison, traveled with them to stand with Mansa during her wedding ceremony. Mansa's sister Kos also came from Springfield, Virginia, to represent the bride's family in Ghana. The day after, the newlyweds went with Diana and Kos to the Junkenuu Carnival. After seeing Diana and Kos off at the Miami International Airport, Mansa and DeJohn drove off to New Orleans to hang out with Tyrone, the groom's college roommate and best friend, relishing good eats and frequenting jazz and blues dives. Upon their return to Madison, Mansa's two best friends,

Ndyanao from Tanzania, who was in the program with her, and Diana, threw a party for the newlyweds. Mansa took her qualifying exams five months pregnant with their first child, Kofi Amu, who was born during the summer holidays on June 7, 1985, five days after to the couple's first anniversary. Maame Mensima was born on December 12, 1986, exactly a week to Mansa's birthday. With Mansa's proposal to work on the topic, "Ayi Kwei Armah: An African Worldview in Fiction." Approved, she continued to read and research her dissertation topic while still teaching the two introductory classes assigned to her.

DeJohn was receiving a decent salary, and Mansa was earning some income from teaching. So, she could send the two children to Auntie Comfort, a Ghanaian woman babysitting infants and toddlers. When Kofi Amu turned two and Maame Mensima six months, DeJohn interviewed for a Management Analyst position with Dade County Public Schools. Though he got the position, he was reluctant to accept it because he was worried to leave Mansa alone with the two young kids. But she egged him on. "Eagle Heights is a secure, family friendly complex. And my two besties, Ndyanao and Diana, are just a stone throw away. Also, their teenage girls, Madaka and Frema, love to babysit our kids. They come here to play with them, take them to play at the playground, or take them home when their parents are around. And, of course, there is Mama Comfort, our regular, reliable, Ghanaian babysitter. The Miami job pays more; and taking the job will take us out of this freezing hell back to the Sunshine State and near your family. And you know Miami reminds me of my home country, Ghana. We will be back near the Atlantic Ocean."

DeJohn started working at the School Board on August 1, 1987 and came home for two weeks during the Christmas holidays. Then in early April, 1988, he came to move his family to Miami. Relocating was harder than Mansa had anticipated.

Though Miami reminded her so much of Ghana, she had to face the hard reality that she knew no one outside her husband's family. Extrovert Mansa became a recluse in Miami, going nowhere unless she was with DeJohn. Aggravating her situation was the fact that for the first time in her adult life, she had neither a teaching position nor an affiliation to any university in the area, though Miami had a good number of them, both state and private. Not being one to mope for long, Mansa, soon tired of the lackluster life she was living and snapped out of the ennui usurping her vivacity. Determined to familiarize herself with her new world, she started with a visit to her neighborhood library which, to her delight, was barely five miles from their home. The Chief Librarian, Ella Smith, told her about a Black Heritage & Book Club that met at the library every fortnight on Friday nights from 8:00 p.m. to 9:45 p.m. Their next meeting was scheduled for that Friday that week.

The Heritage & Book Club members welcomed Mansa with open arms. It was at that meeting that she caught up with the Miami *Niggaratti, the* Black Intelligentsia. The first meeting she attended was efficaciously, the group's first meeting after Spring Break-the one at which the agenda for the rest of the year is planned, in addition to suggesting topics/ideas for the club's featured summer public lecture that is co-sponsored with the library. Mansa's proposal to present on Toni Morrison's *Beloved* was unanimously accepted as the club's choice for the featured lecture.

Mansa's presentation on the topic, "The *Kwasamba* Syndrome: African Spirituality and Morrison's *Beloved*," marked her integration into the Miami intellectual and cultural world. Well attended and well received, and followed by a sumptuous reception, Mansa met people who became her mainstay in Miami One such person was Dr. Ross, a University of Miami Administrator and Professor of Women's Studies, who gave Mansa her card and invited her to come to UM Campus ASAP to see about a potential teaching position. Renee, a female student from UM, offered to take Mansa the next day to the campus. Kwame Adjei, a Ghanaian attending Miami Dade College, exchanged numbers with Mansa. He promised to introduce her to the Ghanaian community and to a Yoruba elder and Priest of Obatala, Chief Ajamu. And Raining Deer, a club member, invited Mansa to a family-friendly party by *Imani Um Nommo* Black Writers the next Friday to read from her poetry. African drummers at the party and Ella approached Mansa about offering Ghanaian Dance and Storytelling at the Library. Considering the offer a way to normalize her life and expose her children to Ghanaian culture, she chose Wednesday nights at eight for Dance Class and Saturday noon for Storytelling.

On Monday, as soon as Mansa and Renee arrived at Dr. Ross's office, she called Zack Bowen, the Chair of the English Department. "Zack, I am sending the one I told you about. She's on her way." Renee walked with Mansa to the English Department office and returned to Dr. Ross's office to wait for Mansa. Zack Bowen, being a straight-shooter, offered Mansa a Visiting Assistant Professor position that would start in the spring right away. Caught completely off guard by Zack Bowen's straight-forwardness, Mansa asked when she could interview for the position.

"The position is yours. Mansa, you come highly recommended by Ross. And your resume backs Ross up."

Emboldened by Zack Bowen's directness, Mansa asked, "Is it possible for me to get something for the fall?"

"The only available classes are Freshmen Comp for adjunct pay — a lot of work for chump-change."

"I'll take it. My greatest need at this point is gaining access to a research library."

"Mary, I am sending Mansa to you. Assign her two comp classes, including everything she needs. Mansa, I will see you in fall."

Contemplating how smoothly Zack Bowen had handled hiring her cradled Mansa in a sea of calm as she made her way back to Dr. Ross's office. Dr. Ross took Mansa and Renee to a French Bistro in Coral Gables to celebrate. DeJohn also took Mansa and her children out to celebrate as soon as he got home from work.

Energized by her active community life and impending return to the academy, time just flew. Mansa's spirit soared upon realizing that she was pregnant. Always invigorated by her pregnancies, the school year advanced effortlessly. Knowing the baby would be born after the spring semester, Mansa didn't have to worry about the academic year becoming interrupted by the baby's birth. Ndyanao Maylena was born on June 8, 1989, at North Shore Hospital in North Miami. Mansa was happy to have an African American obstetrician for the first time since she started making babies in America, even if she had to go through a Cesarean section like with her other two.

Having her baby Ndyanao early June, Mansa would have ample time to bond with her new baby and to spend quality time with her family. There would also be time to find a babysitter for the new baby and a preschool for the two older children prior to the beginning of the 1989/90 academic year. Fortunately, Chief Ajamu told her about a Black-owned school, comprising a nursery, a preschool, and a primary school that was just a mile from her home. Mansa fell in love with the name, "Rainbow Nursery and Preparatory School," and the miracle of having all her three children under one establishment. When she visited the school with her children and saw how well the two older ones meshed with the other children, she registered all three of hers to start two weeks before she would have to start the new academic year.

Mansa truly loved teaching at the University of Miami. Zack Bowen, her chair, was a gem, and she got on well with members of her Department. Being a private institution, majority of the students had good reading and writing skills. Her two Composition classes, not taking up much of her time, left her ample time for Mansa to work on her dissertation and to continue being active in the community. Her dance classes and storytelling at the library also provided avenue for Ghanaian Dance and Ananse Stories to gain recognition in the community.

Mansa got pregnant with her fourth child during her third year at UM, but she didn't miss a beat. The baby would be born during the summer when Mansa would be done with her teaching and other work-related obligations. Immersed in her new life, time had flown by so fast that the new baby's birth was imminent. The dance troupe and writers' group teamed up to organize a baby shower for Mansa. Chief Ajamu also assured her he would perform the baby's naming and outdooring ceremony.

Early morning on Tuesday, May 21, 1991, the scheduled day for the Cesarean, the expectant parents headed to North Shore Hospital. Once given the epidural, Mansa became groggy by the time she was being wheeled into the theater, with DeJohn beside her, holding on to her hand. Despite being groggy, Mansa eagerly awaited the nurse bringing her newborn and placing her on her mother's warm stomach for mother and child to start bonding. Hazy but awake, she lay there envisioning the tugging and the pulling going on without her experiencing raw pain. Suddenly, she became apprehensive, sensing some commotion going on behind the curtain.

Dr. Adams was urgently issuing orders to the assisting nurses. DeJohn moved from her side and went behind the screen that had been erected over her stomach to shield her from the bloody business of the Cesarean. Mansa became frantic. She hadn't heard her baby cry. She knew the baby had been pulled out of her. Why was no one bringing her baby for her?

"What's going on? Where is my baby?" DeJohn appeared from behind the curtain, took Mansa's hand and said softly, "Please be patient."

Mansa started wailing: "I want my baby. Please God, don't let my baby die. Something is wrong with my baby. Oh, my God, my baby is dying."

Mansa was hysterical even though DeJohn was right there beside her, cradling her. One of the two assisting nurses gave her an injection which should calm her down some. But Mansa grabbed her hand, whimpering, "Can I please see my baby ... Please?"

The nurse nodded sympathetically. "Soon. Mrs. Jones; soon."

After a lifetime, a different nurse brought the baby from behind the tent. Mansa screamed as soon as she saw the baby.

"No, that *is not* my baby." She said nothing more, seeming to have passed out.

Doctor Adams finally emerged from behind the tent. He summoned his calmest, most sympathetic voice and took Mansa's hand in his.

"Mrs. Jones, please don't panic. The baby has a cleft lip and palate on the left side of her upper lip. She has extra digits on the extremities, and she has difficulty breathing. She has to be taken to the ICU right away. Her defects could be cosmetic, in which case, plastic surgery can fix her defects. But we will not know until we have run some tests. Don't worry. The pediatric doctors will take great care of her. I am putting in an order for a chromosome test on you. That will let us know whether the defects are cosmetic or not. The ICU pediatric nurses and doctors will take excellent care of your baby."

With all the commotion over the baby, Mansa had forgotten she herself had been cut open for the baby to be pulled out of her. She was freezing and burning up all at once and in excruciating pain but wouldn't ask for help. In her demented mind, the cleft had become a crater that had swallowed the baby's whole face and head. When she closed her eyes trying to remember what the baby looked like, all she could conjure up was an abyss.

After what seemed an interminably long time, Mansa came to in her hospital room. DeJohn who would normally stay with her was not around. In her frenzied mind all she could conjure up was the searing pain from the Cesarean cut that had usurped her whole being, and the crater eating up her baby's face and head. Fear, shame, and anguish were Mansa's constant companions. No medication could mitigate her agony. She had sunk into a dark hole where she could remember nothing distinctly. She wanted to die from failing to bring a healthy child into the world. She did not want to be the mother of that baby with the gaping hole where a beautiful face should be. She felt like such a loser, one whose womb had turned into a deathtrap no longer capable of nurturing life.

That night Baba came to see her. He brought her an African violet and a black pebble that fitted into her palm to hold on to and told her not to worry about anything. "It is all in the hands of God and the ancestors," were his parting words. Morning Dew also called her that evening and told her not to worry about a thing. She and the dancers would get her house ready for Mansa's return.

With the three children, despite the Cesarean, she would insist on going by the nursery to see her baby on the day she came into the world. On this occasion, she found herself afraid to see the baby. It took three whole days for her to finally make it to the ICU. Even then it took DeJohn showing up with a wheel chair, picking her up from the bed, wheeling her to the ICU, and leaving her in front of her baby's crib without a word. Mansa sat there sobbing hysterically, afraid to look at the baby. She looked so forlorn the nurse let her be. Fifteen whole minutes into Mansa's arrival, she finally nodded at the nurse who came promptly, picked up Baby Jones from her bassinet and placed her in her mother's arms.

Mansa continued sobbing silently. Eventually, she garnered enough courage to glance at her baby. What she saw blew her mind. Her child had a full head of curly black hair, unlike most of the bald-headed babies in the unit. What had appeared to Mansa as a crater was nothing more than a cut, about half-an-inch long, on the left side of her baby's lip and palate. Her baby had a face, intact, whole and even beautiful with only a little deformity around the upper lip and palate. But the rest of her face was undamaged and beautiful.

Mansa stayed with her baby, holding and rocking her gently. "Can I nurse my baby?"

"I wish. But with the cleft, she can't grip your nipple in order to suck breast milk. But once the milk is dropped down her throat, she can swallow it. She has a healthy appetite."

"Can you teach me to feed this baby with special needs? I really would love to feed her."

"Sure. I'll get her bottle ready. This is a special nipple—one longer than the conventional nipple. When the milk is dropped down her throat, she can swallow it. I am right here if you need me."

"Wow! You have gusto. Great appetite. I see you love to eat. Nana, I am sorry I didn't come to you sooner. I can't wait to take you home." Mansa was in the ICU still rocking Nana when DeJohn arrived. She put Nana back in her bassinet gently.

"Thank you, nurse. I'll see you tomorrow."

The mother continued to go to the hospital every day to care for her baby when the mother got discharged five days after the Cesarean. She also took CPR at the hospital in anticipation of Baby Jones' discharge. But her heart ached when the eight day came and her baby was still in the hospital. Chief Ajamu consoled her. "I will pour libation to the Almighty and the Ancestors on the eight day. And we will go on with the ceremony on the Tuesday following her discharge.

Friday of the baby's second week, the parents were summoned to a meeting with the resident pediatrician. She showed them pictures of former cleft children who had been 'fixed up' by plastic surgery. "This one is my now eight-year old. He was born with the same problem your child has. There is hope for your child."

"Wow! So you have experienced what we are dealing with? Your son doesn't look anything like my child does now."

"Just don't lose hope. Here is a package for her discharge, including a referral to a plastic surgeon in Miami. You have been doing such a marvelous job taking care of Baby Jones. You are taking her home today. Don't forget to call the plastic surgeon ASAP."

Though somewhat apprehensive, Mansa considered the baby's discharge more auspicious. She called Chief as soon as they got home.

"Great. The naming and outdooring ceremony can take place on Tuesday, the day of the week on which she was born."

God being so good, Mansa's sister Ewura Ekua and her two children, Denu and Sika, came from Ghana to visit three days after the baby was discharged. Their timing could not have been more propitious.

Early Tuesday morning, Baba arrived at the home of Mansa and DeJohn accompanied by his sister Yeye; his wife Iya Shangode; and Yeye's three children who were age-mates of the Jones' three. Also present were Morning Dew, eight dancers, among them Onisegi, and three drummers. The children went to the all-purpose room in the back part of the house to play.

Chief cast the divination cowries three times and stopped. He beckoned the parents and Ewura Ekua to step with him into the backyard.

"This baby has a precarious life-path. She is an *Abiku; Kwasamba*. The cleft lip and palate and extra digits are a manifestation of transitory existence. You will have to be vigilant. She is at this point straddling both worlds and can slip back into the other world." Chief stopped a dramatic minute and then asked: "What name have you chosen for her?" Mansa was silent, pensive, looking at nothing and no one. Minutes later, she pulled herself out of her stupor.

"Sunkwa; Nana Araba Sunkwa. Sunkwa is the name of my mother's mother. It means to 'seek life;' also to 'lament your mortality.' That should be an appropriate name for a baby who has one leg in the world of the living and the other in *Samanadzi*, the Ancestral world, Chief. Araba is the Mfantse day-name for one born on Tuesday. And since Sunkwa is my maternal grandmother's name, she has to wear the honorific name Nana. Her full name will be Nana Araba Sunkwa; Nana because that is my grandmother's name; and Araba because she is born on Tuesday."

Mansa was thankful the baby had been discharged so the naming ceremony could take place, even if it was taking place two weeks later than customary. In a strange way, Chief Ajamu divining that their baby was a *kwasamba* somehow fortified Mansa. She knew a *kwasamba* child could die; but she felt prepared to take on the challenge of mothering this child in a manner that the hospital doctors with their faith in plastic surgery and their assumption that Sunkwa's defects were cosmetic could neither give her peace nor strength. The pediatric doctors 'missed road' in considering Sunkwa's cleft to be merely cosmetic. Plastic surgery would not be the fix-all and end-all for her Nana Araba Sunkwa. Her life is what it should be. God and the Ancestors have spoken.

Three days after the naming ceremony, the hospital called.

"This is the Jones residence."

"Can you come back to the hospital? The chromosome test is back."

The couple bundled the baby up and drove back to the hospital. They were taken to the same room where they had been shown the repaired clefts.

"Baby Jones is a Trisomy Thirteen."

"What does that mean?"

"Her 13th chromosome is defective. Her condition is fatal."

"How can that be? You're telling me her condition cannot be fixed? That cannot be."

Three days later, Nana Araba Sunkwa turned blue while gulping her milk. Mansa performed CPR to revive her. Life continued semi-smoothly for four days. Then she choked on her milk again and turned blue. Mansa performed CPR and she was revived. However, it happened again—three times the next day. So DeJohn called an ambulance, while Mansa was performing the third CPR. The parents left with the baby. While in Triage, she stopped breathing. Mansa rushed to the pediatrician in Triage.

"Oh, it's you. What do you want here? Don't you understand she is a NOLIFE? Hospitals don't waste *resources* on NOLIFES."

"Please Doctor. This is my baby you are calling a NOLIFE. She will die if she doesn't get help. PLEASE DO SOMETHING."

"Oh, you are afraid of watching her die in your arms anh? She came out of your womb. You are her mother. Take her home." She turned to the next patient making it clear she was done with Mansa and her baby palaver.

Shaking like a leaf on a windy fall day, Mansa would have dropped on the floor with Sunkwa in her arms if DeJohn hadn't caught her. With one arm wrapped around her and the other around their baby, he steered them towards a phone outside Triage. He called Dr. Simpson, their pediatrician.

"Don't worry. Your baby is not going to be thrown out of the hospital. I'll take care of that."

Upon Dr. Simpson's intervention, a nurse eventually appeared, took the baby from the father and asked the parents to follow her. She stopped outside the nurses' station, handed the baby back to her mother and disappeared. She finally reappeared with a bassinet, placed it against a wall in the hallway, and told DeJohn to put his baby in the bassinet. Mansa's eyes widened. Before she could say anything, the nurse explained.

"She has been outside the sterilized environment of the ICU. Cannot keep her with the other newborns. We have to protect the neonates. But don't worry. Your baby will be cared for. She is after all where the nurses can see her."

Mansa boohooed all the way home. Dr. Simpson called first thing in the morning to tell them the hospital will find an extended care facility to which Nana Araba Sunkwa could be transferred.

When she checked on her baby, it was evident no nurse had been assigned to Baby Sunkwa's care. The mother asked for a fresh diaper, washcloth, and antiseptic baby wash and cleaned her baby and changed her diaper and clothes. Mansa continued to go to the hospital each day to care for Nana Araba Sunkwa, while anxiously awaiting word about locating an extended care place to which their baby could be sent.

Finally, on a Wednesday, three weeks later, when the parents showed up to care for their baby, they were directed to an office to do the paper work necessary for their baby's transfer to an extended care facility in Davie in Broward County. Mansa accompanied the baby in the ambulance; and DeJohn followed in their car, to what would be Sunkwa's new home.

The facility was a nice, clean place with caring nurses, set up to accommodate terminally-ill children. The whole family, including the children, could go visit with Nana Araba Sunkwa anytime. On the drive back home, the parents picked up the three children at Auntie's. Then they went by their favorite fish market and bought fried snapper and conch salad. Mansa stayed home with the children the following day.

On the third day, she told DeJohn she would go to UM with the children to her office, and then take them with her to visit Nana Araba Sunkwa. On the way to her office with the children, they stopped at the house of Betty Jean, Mansa's friend/actor and dancing sister. Not having seen Mansa and the children, since the naming and outdooring ceremony, she was eager to spend time with them.

Mansa had barely finished reading her mail and picking

up her books for the approaching semester when the office phone rang. It was DeJohn. "Can you meet me at Sunkwa's extended care place? I am already there, so you'll have to drive there yourself." Without him saying anything more, Mansa knew she would have to ask Betty Jean, if she could accompany her back to her house to stay with her children, while she dashed down to Davie to meet DeJohn.

When Mansa got there, she knew even before she was told anything that Sunkwa had passed on. DeJohn was holding her in his arms. Her woes finally over, she looked peaceful like one in deep sleep. Mansa sat beside DeJohn and he handed her the baby. The only giveaway was that beads of cold sweat had bathed her whole body and her body continued to grow cold; very cold. And she was starting to turn blue. The two parents sat holding her, passing her from one to the other, while a nurse talked to them about funeral arrangements. Knowing nothing about such matters, Mansa called Chief Ajamu. "Because Sunkwa is a *Kwasamba*, burying her might not be a good idea. After all, we bury things we want to grow. But we do not want a *Kwasamba/Abiku* to perpetuate the cycle of being born only to die prematurely and keep repeating the cycle of repeated births resulting in sudden deaths."

Chief recommended cremation and suggested a number of funeral homes that were more sympathetic to African funeral rites. He asked Mansa and DeJohn to come see him once they were done with the arrangements. Mr. Poitier, pleased to be contacted by his former student, agreed to take charge of the cremation for a very reasonable fee.

Mansa, especially, was happy with the choice of cremation. Considering she wasn't from this part of the world, she couldn't bear to have a vital part of herself buried under American soil.

When the bereaved parents got to African Temple and Marketplace, Baba poured libation and performed some rituals in the name of Sunkwa. The women prepared a cleansing bath for Mansa and laid out a change of clothes for her. Following that, some food was brought to give thanks to God and the Ancestors for releasing Sunkwa from her earthly woes and to celebrate her sojourn in their midst. Chief advised the couple, especially the mother, not to grieve too much. When Mansa and DeJohn were ready, he would complete the rituals of transition for Sunkwa.

The following day, Mansa's sister dancers came to the house. They told Mansa and DeJohn to leave the children and go to the movies, or go do something fun and not worry about the children. Abena, a dancer with young children the age of Mansa's, took the children for the day and kept them for the night too. The other sister dancers cleaned the house and cooked before they left. Throughout the following week, one or the other member of Mansa's community of friends dropped in to express their condolences.

Within a week, Mansa felt she was strong enough to bring closure to Sunkwa's passing. So DeJohn called Chief Ajamu to request if he could complete Sunkwa's transition rituals on Friday. Late Friday morning of the following week, the Jones family drove to the temple to pick up Chief Ajamu. Then they stopped at the Funeral Home. Mansa and the children stayed in the car, while the two men went inside the funeral home to pick up Sunkwa's ashes. Then, they drove to the Miami River.

At the bank of the river, on a very quiet street, Chief asked DeJohn to park the car. They got out. Chief picked up the ashes and whatever else he was carrying in his duffle/medicine bag. Leaving his slippers on the bank of the river, he walked a few feet, halfway down his thighs, into the water.

First, he poured libation, then recited some incantations. After that, he emptied Sunkwa's ashes into the river. Mansa, somehow, felt reassured that the ashes would flow through the Miami River into the Atlantic Ocean, and Sunkwa will make the journey back home to her motherland. Somehow seeing the ashes poured into the river and having Chief Ajamu perform the rituals gave a sense of closure to Sunkwa's death.

The Jones family and Chief left the Miami River and went back to African Temple and Marketplace, where some of the members from the dance troupe, and other well-wishers, had gathered with food and drinks. Mansa's sister dancers circled her in dance and the drums played to speed Sunkwa on her journey to *Samanadzi*, the world of her ancestors.

Despite her grief at losing her baby, Nana Araba Sunkwa, Mansa felt it deep within her womb that no matter where else she moved to, Miami would always be home to her; for a part of her had been left there, feeding its rivers and ocean.

H. Oby Okolocha

H. Oby Okolocha, Ph.D. is an Associate Professor of English, Department of English and Literature, University of Benin, Benin City, Edo State, Nigeria. Dr. Okolocha's scholarly interests are in drama, particularly in literature dealing with gender, feminism, trauma, conflict and social justice, areas in which she has publications in scholarly journals inside and outside Africa. She has also published short stories and poetry in *Reflections: An Anthology of New Work by African Women Poets*, *Journal of the African Literature Association of America* (JALA), and *Matatu*. Dr. Okolocha is a member of the African Literature Association (ALA), African Studies Association (ASA), Literary Society of Nigeria (LSN), and Association of African Women Scholars (AAWS).

Thirteen

The Londoner Goes Home

THE NIGHT WAS WET, AND THE MOON was in hiding, when the sharp metallic ambulance Volvo station wagon crawled to a halt in front of the narrow entrance beside the stained white house standing along the old, curved street of inland town, Onitsha, followed closely by an aging Toyota Sienna. As if on cue, crying, wailing, praises and welcome chants filled the air simultaneously, competing for attention and confusing each other.

"Shaka the Zulu! London Boy! Onye Ije nnọ ọ!" (Traveler, welcome!)!

"Nwoke-ọcha nnọ ọ (white man, welcome)!! Onye obodo Oyibo" (*Diasporic person*)!

"Ụwa bụ afịa! Onye zụsia ọ na!" (*The world is a market; you go home when you have finished buying!*)

From the car behind, Akuerika watched the crowd gather around the ambulance, while Akunnia struggled to open the boot of the Volvo to reach his older brother. Akunnia and Chiejina had not been on speaking terms for almost 20 years, but this was death. Whoever continues to have a quarrel with a dead man was at fault and that is because the man was no longer there to defend himself. Besides, she knew that Akunnia understood that this was *the* opportunity. And *the* opportunity will not come a second time. Then the boot opened slowly upwards and there he was. The brown and gold mahogany casket gleamed in the dim light. She watched the crowd jostle to get a closer look like someone in a trance. She watched Akunnia slowly lift the cover of the casket as if in slow motion and just then it came from nowhere, the shrill lamentation that pierced the fog in her mind!

"Ụnụ nụkwalụ na Chiejina, nnukwu nwa Obiọzọ a naa

nmụọ?
Chiejina nwa Obịọzọ a naa nmụọ!"
(*Have you heard that Chiejina, the great son of Obịọzọ, has gone to the spirit world?*)

"Ụwa etie oko oko o, ụnụ afụkwalụ na onye nọsia n'enu ụwa ọ naa nmụọ!" (2ce)
(*The world cries out, with a reminder that whoever comes into the world must return to the spirit world*)

Somehow, the shrill voice calmed the turmoil in Akuerika's mind as she sat there, watching, waiting and remembering. She remembered that the same type of ambulance-like Volvo had taken them to Lagos to board the Nigerian Airways flight to London forty-five years ago. The years flitted through her mind like television commercials as she watched the crowd outside. She knew that they had not yet realized that she was there. She took a deep breath and turned to Chude, her stepson, sitting across the back seat. They both knew it was time. She placed her hand on the door handle, the two back doors opened at the same time. The click of shutting doors disrupted the regularized and confused outpouring of varying sentiments.

The frenzy came to a stop in an untidy choreography as if electricity went off, came back on dimly and went off again. Then silence! It was the silent transmission of pressurized mixed feelings. The stares were intense, angry, gleeful and calculating. Chiejina, the fallen returnee, got a reprieve from prying eyes and poking fingers making sure that 'London Boy' had returned a complete man. The silence was a respite from the calculations... She watched calculations shift. The man who emerged from the other side of the car provided another subplot. She watched as faces made silent conversations with each other. Who would this be? It began to click. She saw the wonder.

"Could this muscular tattooed man be Chude, their brother's first son who was almost 60 years of age?"

"This gangster had come to bury a titled father?"

Akuerika watched Akunnia decide that this had to be Chude. The resemblance to Chiejina was uncanny. The air had thickened with misgivings and Chude's insolent stare spoke volumes. Akuerika's feeling of dread increased. Akunnia broke the silence:

"Thank you, Iyawo, for bringing back our brother to rest with his father and brothers in the family *Iba*."

Akuerika knew that Akunnia would never let his anger show. She knew that he hated her husband, hated him now in death as much as he had hated him in his lifetime. Like most who had relatives abroad, Akunnia thought his brother Chiejina had not taken care of the people at home half as much as he should have done. Yes, she knew Chiejina's reputation as a miserly person. She knew that his relatives often asked themselves: "What was the use of having a relative abroad if there was no benefit? He might as well have stayed at home!" But then, these people did not know that he had been much more generous to them than he had been at home. Akunnia's voice came again, directing Chude and a few other young men to take Chiejina into his father's *Iba*. The rest of them trailed into the decrepit bungalow. He didn't even have a house of his own in the homestead. The intrigues would begin now. It was so whenever *onye obodo oyibo* returned in the golden box with the sparkling white satin bed, but that was not important now. What mattered was that despite his name, Chiejina – *may the sun not set* – the Londoner had come home at sunset!

Fourteen

Travel Ban

THE SEAT WAS TOO TIGHT FOR HIS tall frame. He had barely enough room without any number of shopping bags. He gave her a short derisive glare from deep dark eyes that were irritated with her for having that many bags cluttering up the narrow space. She glared back with eyes that wondered why her bags were his business. Apart from the rustling sounds they made as she shifted to arrange them, how did her bags disturb him?

"Aah! These superior, snotty types," she thought. Why didn't he buy a first-class seat, if he didn't want rustling bags?"

A surreptitious glance noted the silver Rolex, the expensive-looking leather wallet and the manicured beard incongruous with short cultivated dreadlocks, the bold T-shirt and the tattoo on his right wrist. Classy and common? A footballer? An actor? A terrorist? A pirate? Who was he? She wondered.

"Well?" he asked.

Uzoaku was too dark to blush at being caught stealing glances at a strange man, but she was embarrassed, so she took refuge in silence. Aware of his masculinity and women taking a second look, she thought. Probably someone's loose treasure! She turned her eyes back to the narrow aisle. If their flight hadn't been cancelled and passengers distributed to other airlines, she wouldn't be sitting next to Mr. Dark Macho here.

After long minutes of trying to keep her eyes fixated on the aisle, she decided to read. But she would need to rustle her bags again to get her book. To hell with Mr. Macho! She would rustle her bags all she wanted. She had paid full fare for her seat! With determination, she loosened her seatbelt, bent forward and groped under her seat for her polythene bags and hauled them up to her laps. She searched out her book and could almost hear him wondering if she didn't know what the hand luggage compartment was for.

"You should have reserved a seat for these things if you don't want them in the hand luggage compartment," he smirked, giving her packages speaking glare as she tried to tuck a squishy bag-full of assorted items under her seat.

She stiffened at the disdain in his tone. How had two strangers started this silent quarrel in such a short time? She resolved to ignore him. In Nigeria, it is said that 'silence is the best answer for a fool'...He had to be a fool to dislike her without cause, so silence it was going to be! Well, it was going to be a long flight to Jackson Airport, Atlanta.

She leaned back in her seat, opened her novel with determination, but concentration would not come. After minutes of staring blankly at the pages of her book, she closed her book, put it on her lap and closed her eyes. She would sleep! And it looked like sleep would be more cooperative than reading, but just as she was settling into a doze, she jerked awake, disoriented again.

What was it that had woken her? She wondered. Then she realized that the plane was jerking like someone dancing to some African cultural rhythm!

"Oh! My God!"

As if in reaction to her exclamation, the plane calmed down, but only for a few minutes, it seemed. Then, it dived in and out of the clouds in bumpy movements as if it was driving across gallops and potholes on Lagos-Benin highway. Were there bad roads in the sky? She wondered. She stole a glance at the bearded pirate next to her. She wondered if he felt any apprehension. She decided that he couldn't possibly be afraid of an unruly plane ride... he looked indomitable and it irritated her that she was taking too much notice of him. But, as the plane continued to stagger through the clouds in the manner of a man staggering out of an Irish pub, her mind began to stagger in concord with the movement of the plane.

"American Delta airplane with 90% African passengers staggering like some drunken sailors?"

"Why was the door of the cockpit always locked, if there was no mischief going on in there?"

"Had someone arranged a suicide bomber to rid America of one plane-load of Africans?"

Unconsciously, she began to murmur:

"Hail Mary, full of grace..."

He turned to look at her and she expected him to make some scathing comment, but to her surprise, he joined her prayers:

"Blessed are you among women and blessed is the fruit of your womb, Jesus! Holy Mary, Mother of God, pray for us sinners, now and at the hour of death, Amen." In unison, they prayed: "Our Father, who art in heaven, hallowed be thy name..."

Ten minutes later, walls of animosity dissolved in their session of murmured prayers. She asked:

"Are you Catholic?"

"Very much so," he answered, drawing out the Catholic scapula round his neck.

A scapula, dreadlocks, and a tattoo? She wondered. What a treacherous combination! But, she needed a friend for this precarious plane ride and her mind clutched at the tiny laminated picture and scribble on the scapula hanging on a tiny cloth rope around his neck. Yes, tattoo and dreadlocks or not, the tiny cloth rope testified to good righteous behavior and her spirits lifted. A brother in Christ! Besides, their prayers had taken effect and the plane was becoming increasingly calm.

"I am sorry that I was rude about your bags earlier," he said.

"Apology accepted. Let's forget about it," she said, smiling slightly.

"What's your name?" he asked.

"Ụzọakụ Onyechikpụrụ."

"I am called Sadodo, but my baptismal name is Clinton Chikpụzirim. Our surnames are similar; you must be from Imo State?" he asked.

"Yes, from Ehime, Mbaino," she replied.

"And I am from Orlu, a neighboring town. You are really my sister!"

Old animosity passed away and a new brotherhood and sisterhood was born as quickly as the animosity had formed. The hours to Atlanta passed quickly in the harmony of exchanged stories. Ụzọakụ learned that Sadodo was a footballer as well as a basketball player that had been admitted into one of those colleges in America on a basketball scholarship. Nigeria did not recognize the importance of sports, as America did. So, a number of talented athletes in Nigeria were, like Sadodo, leaving the country in search of greener pastures. In return, Sadodo learned that Ụzọakụ had studied Accounting at Imo State University, Owerri, but had gone on to do nursing because everyone knew that nursing is the gateway to riches in England and America.

They arrived at Jackson airport without further temptation. Inside the building, sign posts asked those with US passports to go in one direction, EU citizens in another direction and 'other passports' in yet another direction. Ụzọakụ saw that their queue, those holding 'other passports,' was thrice as long as the US passport holders' line, indicating the large number of traffic to the USA. She estimated that it would take one or two hours to get through immigration, but unlike some others on the queue, she was not irritated. She knew what it had taken to get there! Sadodo also looked prepared to wait.

Nearly two hours later and two lines away, they were nearer the immigration cubicles. Ụzọakụ could now observe the people in front and the immigration officials behind the glass cubicles clearly. About nineteen clearing cubicles in all, mostly empty. Five of the cubicles were attending to those with US passports, three to EU citizens and four cubicles attending to the long line of 'other passports.' Sadodo, now a brother, was right in front. She noted that the immigration officers were mostly people of other races; Mexicans, Hispanics, Blacks, and only a couple of white people wearing the same dark pants or skirt and a blue shirt. And apart from the cat-eyed Asian-looking girl in cubicle nine, whose face wore an honest smile, the other faces wore variants of the one look. Faces that said, "You better have a good reason to be in America!" The structure of questions was about the same, too.

"Where are you from?"

"London"

Do you hold British citizenship?

"Yes," and the questions would be brief, and the square-faced immigration officer would say: "Welcome to America!"

But, for young men of below 50 years of age and whose answer to the rapid "where are you from?" is Nigeria, the initial verdict was invariably: "Step aside!" Having watched this scenario repeat itself monotonously from the queue, it was their turn too soon.

"Next!" The immigration officer called out and Sadodo hurried to the cubicle, which faced the queue directly.

"Where are you from?"

"Rwanda!" Uzoaku's shock was overshadowed by fear for the doubt that flitted across the face of the balding, slightly overweight officer. What on earth was happening here? She hadn't taken note of the color of the passport he held, but she knew for sure that he was from Orlu in Nigeria. She held her breath as the officer stared at Sadodo with the concentration of a priest about to hear confession. She squirmed uneasily on her feet, waiting for the inevitable "Step aside!"

"Recite the Rwandan national anthem," she heard the officer command him.

She watched Sadodo stand upright, cross his right hand across his chest, and sing solemnly:

"Onye kelu uwa nekwaa ikpele m n'ala,

Chineke ị dị nma, Chineke ị dị nma...
Onye bi n'igwe, nekwaa ikpele m n'ala,
Chineke ị dị nma ooo...!"

Recognizing a responsible law-abiding citizen, the immigration officer nodded, stamped the passport deftly and passed it through the small space under the glass.

"Welcome to America!"

Next!